M. E.

PREFECTS OF THE CHALET SCHOOL

ELINOR M BRENT-DYER

Girls Gone By Publishers

COMPLETE AND UNABRIDGED

Published by

Girls Gone By Publishers
4 Rock Terrace
Coleford
Bath
Somerset
BA3 5NF

First published by W & R Chambers Ltd 1970
This edition published 2007
Text and Chalet School characters © Girls Gone By Publishers
Preface © Helen McClelland 2007
Prefects—the Contract © Clarissa Cridland 2007
The Little Company of Mary: The Blue Nuns © Ann Mackie-Hunter
    2007
The Chalet School Series: an Introduction © Clarissa Cridland 2002
Elinor M Brent-Dyer: a Brief Biography © Clarissa Cridland 2002
Publishing History © Clarissa Cridland 2007
Appendix I © Laura Hicks 2007
Appendix II © Ruth Jolly 2007
Appendix III © Ruth Jolly 2007
Design and Layout © Girls Gone By Publishers 2007

Typeset in England by AJF
Printed in England by Antony Rowe Limited

ISBN 978-1-84745-021-0

"Get up Margot!" Miss Annersley exclaimed. *"And who let that dog in here?"*

PREFACE: PHYLLIS AND *PREFECTS*

Prefects of the Chalet School, the last of the series, was not published until March 1970, six months after the author's death. The contract to publish *Prefects* was dated 17 September 1969, which was only three days before Elinor Brent-Dyer died, but it seems clear that the manuscript already existed at this date. Yet there has often been a suggestion that her friend Phyllis Matthewman was partly responsible for helping Elinor with the story, and the question of how far Phyllis was actually involved in this is an intriguing one.

Anyone who attempts to discuss the matter must, from the outset, distinguish between facts and speculation. Almost the only known fact relates to Phyllis having at this stage assisted Elinor by acting as an amanuensis—in other words, sitting at the typewriter to take down the story as dictated by Elinor herself. Phyllis had certainly more skill as a typist than her friend, and may even have learnt touch-typing at some point, whereas EBD's manuscripts had become famous at W & R Chambers for their general untidiness and lack of organisation. This could well have been the main reason for Phyllis's offer to step in, since it doesn't appear that any sight problem prevented Elinor from using the typewriter. Most likely the two would have agreed that, with Phyllis typing and Elinor doing what she was best at—that is, telling the actual story—the manuscript was likely to progress far more quickly.

However, in reading *Prefects* I have always had a strong feeling that there was more than one person involved in telling the story; and this same feeling also persists regarding *Althea Joins the Chalet School* (1969). Between the latter's appearance and that of the previous Chalet title in 1967—*Two Sams at the Chalet School*—there was an uncharacteristically long gap of two years, and it appears that Sydney Matthewman had to exercise considerable patience in getting Elinor to resume the task of continuing the Chalet School saga. If we compare *Two Sams* with *Althea*, I feel there is a distinct variation in approach, and this applies more strongly to the story before *Two Sams*: *Challenge for the Chalet School* (1966), often regarded as among the best of the later titles. But I have to confess right away that this is mainly a 'gut' feeling, and is based partly on having got to know Phyllis pretty well during the five years of our friendship.

She and I had first met in November 1974, and by this time more than five years had passed since Elinor's death. At the time I'd originally felt that all the mysteries about Elinor would quickly be resolved in talking to a very old friend of hers. But by our second meeting it became clear that memory for more recent events was not Phyllis's strong point. At this stage a number of inconsistencies—for example, between the notes made at the first and second interviews—quickly made it plain that she was not a reliable informant about Elinor's more recent days. And, although her reminiscences of early life remained more or less the same, she had clearly never known that Elinor's father had remained alive until 1911.

Besides, there was undoubtedly an element of jealousy in the way Phyllis regarded her friend. From her point of view, it must have been quite difficult to see the continuing fame of the Chalet series, whereas her own efforts in the school-story line had enjoyed only modest success. As the typist of *Prefects,* it would have been so easy for her to influence the line of the story— perhaps just in making suggestions as it went along, or in talking over what a certain person might or might not have done at this point. Elinor was never averse to talking about the characters in her books and their actions; nor do I think that she would ever have troubled to read the manuscript as it proceeded—she plainly didn't often bother with her own!

One answer, in theory, would be to get a computer to work on the story of *Prefects*, and to tell us how many people were involved in writing it—something that computers can do with some accuracy today. In the meanwhile, Ruth Jolly has written a fascinating article on *Prefects of the Chalet School* (see Appendix II), making use of her extensive knowledge of the text and of comparisons within the Chalet series, and her findings will be of enormous interest to all readers.

Helen McClelland
2007

PREFECTS—THE CONTRACT

The contract for *Prefects* is dated 17 September 1969. If one looks closely at it, it seems as though the words 'Seventeenth' and 'September' have been typed in after the contract was signed, both by Chambers and by Elinor Brent-Dyer. This was normal practice at this time, and Chambers had followed this procedure with Elinor since the contract for *The Chalet School Wins the Trick*, dated 10 August 1960. Prior to that, Elinor's contracts with Chambers had been dated when sent to her.

This means that Elinor probably signed the contract a day or two before 17 September. She died on 20 September, only a few days later. The contract is two foolscap pages (an old imperial size, slightly longer than A4), and, as well as signing on the last page, each party initialled the first page (this was standard practice then, and indeed is now). Elinor's initials (right) and signature (below) look very frail.

Note that there is a (postage) stamp underneath the signatures—6d (ie sixpence). This was a legal requirement at that time (though not for much longer). When the contract for *School at the Chalet* was signed the value of the stamp was 2d, and this continued until the contract for *Jo Returns* (dated 4 December 1935) when it was raised to 6d.

There is no clause saying that the typescript for *Prefects* still has to be delivered, and therefore, although the contract does not

MEMORANDUM OF AGREEMENT made this Seventeenth day of September Nineteen Hundred and Sixty-nine between MISS ELINOR M. BRENT-DYER, of Gryphons, 56 Woodlands Road, Redhill, Surrey (hereinafter called "the Author" which expression shall where the context admits include the Author's executors administrators and assigns) of the one part and MESSRS W. & R. CHAMBERS LIMITED, of 11 Thistle Street, Edinburgh EH2 1DG (hereinafter called "the Publisher" which expression shall where the context admits include the Publisher's executors administrators and assigns or successors in business as the case may be) of the other part.

WHEREBY it is agreed as follows:-

1. The Author grants to the Publisher the exclusive rights for the duration of copyright to print and publish her work at present entitled:

PREFECTS OF THE CHALET SCHOOL

specifically say so, it is clear that Elinor had already delivered the complete typescript and Chambers had accepted it. Nowadays this would be spelt out, but in those days much was taken on trust. Contracts were generally still regarded as 'gentlemen's agreements', and this was only just beginning to change when I started in publishing in 1976. (I was trained by a wonderful Contracts Director who would take me through contracts, clause by clause, and explain exactly why my boss should not have agreed to certain things!)

As had been the case since Sydney Matthewman took over as Elinor's agent in the late 1940s, Elinor was paid both a royalty and an advance. From *Island* until *Bride* the advance was £200, but with the publication of *Changes* it was reduced to £150, and it continued at this rate up to and including *Prefects*. The advance covered the first 20,000 copies sold, and after that Elinor was paid a royalty of 5 per cent on the published price. This may not sound a lot of money these days, but it needs to be borne in mind that Elinor was paid £40 for the copyright of *The School at the Chalet*. By 1969 the 'golden age' of the GGBP type of book had really come to an end, and so, in spite of the fact that the Chalet School books bucked this trend, the terms of the contract were not unfair to Elinor.

Clarissa Cridland
2007

PUBLISHING HISTORY

Prefects of the Chalet School was published in hardback by Chambers in 1970, with a frontispiece and dustwrapper by D[orothy] Brook. We have reproduced the frontispiece in this edition, and have used the front of the dustwrapper as our front cover; the spine is shown on the back, where we have also reproduced the text of the original blurb. The 1970 hardback was not reprinted. *Prefects* was published in paperback in 1994 by Armada, with a cover by Gwyneth Jones (see left). This edition was not republished either. To the best of my knowledge there have been no other printings until this GGBP edition.

Text

For this GGBP edition we have used the text of the original hardback edition, and in Appendix I we explain what we have done about its typographical and other errors. We hope we have not added any new ones.

Clarissa Cridland
2007

THE LITTLE COMPANY OF MARY:
THE BLUE NUNS

On pages 102–4 of *Prefects of the Chalet School* the Triplets and Carmela Walther are walking in the School grounds after sorting out Sale needlework items when Margot speaks publicly for the first time of her future intentions after she has completed her medical degree and of her religious vocation: "'I hope to enter the Order of Blue Nuns and from there I shall go to the School of Tropical Nursing and work for my diploma in tropical medicines.'"

The Blue Nuns Margot refers to are The Sisters of the Little Company of Mary, who came to be known as the Blue Nuns from the distinctive blue veils they wear. The order is an English one, founded in Nottingham in 1877 by the Venerable Mary Potter.

Mary was born in Bermondsey, South-east London, in 1847, the youngest of five children and the only daughter. She was greatly influenced by her strong and deeply spiritual mother, who was a convert to Roman Catholicism. William Potter was opposed to his wife's conversion and the children's subsequent baptism into the Roman Catholic Church. Soon after Mary's birth he abandoned his family, and nothing further was heard of him. Mrs Potter moved to Southwark, and in 1865 she moved out of London to Southsea in Hampshire with Mary and her son Thomas.

In Southsea Mary became engaged to a very devout young man, Godfrey King. However, she came to believe that marriage was not to be for her and broke off the engagement. For three years she taught Catholic children, bringing food and comfort to the needy of the parish after classes. Believing herself called to the religious life, at the age of 21 she entered the Sisters of Mercy. However, during her first year she became ill, and she returned home as she thought that her call was not to that particular order.

Although physically frail, in October 1874—after reading, in verse 16 of Chapter 15 of St John's Gospel, Jesus' words 'I chose you, I appointed you to go on and bear fruit, fruit that shall last'— Mary believed that God had called her to nurse and pray for the sick and the dying and to found a company of women dedicated to that purpose. Gradually companions came to join her in her work, and after three years her brother George brought her to the attention of Bishop Edward Bagshawe, the Roman Catholic Bishop of Nottingham.

Bishop Bagshawe gave Mary and her companions, Elizabeth Bryan and Agnes Bray, permission to care for the sick in his diocese. They began on 17 March 1877 in an old warehouse in a very poor area, Hyson Green. Mary dedicated her company of women to the maternal heart of the Blessed Virgin Mary, and named it after the 'little company' of followers who faithfully shared her vigil at the foot of the Cross.

The founding convent of the Little Company of Mary was officially opened by the Bishop on Easter Monday 1877. In May the Company was joined by two trained nurses, Eleanor Smith and Edith Coleridge. On 7 July the five were allowed to don the habit of a sister in a religious order with the blue veil which led to their being known as the Blue Nuns. The nursing habit was white, which made the mid-blue veil very distinctive. This was the habit the public saw. In the convent the habit was black, with a white wimple and a blue veil, and a white cloak for chapel.

The sisters provided midwifery care at a time when infant mortality was high and many mothers died of septicaemia. However, when the Cardinal-Archbishop of Westminster found out he forbade them to continue, as it was against Canon Law for consecrated virgin nuns to deliver babies. The sisters of the Little Company of Mary were able to continue their prenatal care, and they found local women who could attend the births.

Mother Mary Potter made a number of visits to Rome in order

to obtain papal approval for her Order and for its Rule—the sisters' way of living within the authority of the Church as consecrated Religious. This approval was finally given by Pope Leo XIII in 1893, by which time the Little Company of Mary had already established five more houses: two in Italy (a result of Mother Mary's frequent stays there), and one each in Ireland, Australia and the United States. Then, as now, the sisters' aim was to witness to the healing love in Jesus in caring for the poor, the sick, the suffering and the dying. An integral part of their mission is to pray constantly for the suffering and the dying.

The Order continued to spread worldwide, and Mother Mary died on 9 April 1913 in its convent in Rome where she had lived since 1902. In 1997 her remains were removed from the crypt of the Congregation's Calvary Hospital to be brought to England and re-interred in St Barnabas's Cathedral, Nottingham. On 8 February 1988, Pope John Paul II declared Mother Mary Venerable, the first step on the road to canonisation.

The Little Company of Mary flourishes in the 21st century, with hospitals and hospices in many countries. There is an active presence in Africa, and this is probably the mission to which Margot felt called. The Blue Nuns are still in Nottingham, where it all began 130 years ago.

Ann Mackie-Hunter
2007

Further information can be found on the official website of the Little Company of Mary International: http://lcmglobal.org/

THE CHALET SCHOOL SERIES: AN INTRODUCTION

In 1925 W & R Chambers Ltd published *The School at the Chalet*, the first title in Elinor Brent-Dyer's Chalet School series. Forty-five years later, in 1970, the same company published the final title in the series, *Prefects of the Chalet School*. It was published posthumously, EBD (as she is known to her fans) having signed the contract three days before she died. During those 45 years Elinor wrote around 60 Chalet School titles, the School moved from the Austrian Tirol to Guernsey, England, Wales and finally Switzerland, a fan club flourished, and the books began to appear in an abridged paperback format.

How Many Chalet School Titles Are There?
Numbering the Chalet School titles is not as easy as it might appear. The back of the Chambers dustwrapper of *Prefects of the Chalet School* offers a simple list of titles, numbered 1–58. However, no 31, *Tom Tackles the Chalet School*, was published out of sequence (see below), and there were five 'extra' titles, of which one, *The Chalet School and Rosalie*, follows just after *Tom* in the series chronology. In addition, there was a long 'short' story, *The Mystery at the Chalet School*, which comes just before *Tom*. Helen McClelland, EBD's biographer, helpfully devised the system of re-numbering these titles 19a, 19b and 19c (see list on pp24–26).

Further complications apply when looking at the paperbacks. In a number of cases, Armada split the original hardbacks into two when publishing them in paperback, and this meant that the paperbacks are numbered 1–62. In addition, *The Mystery at the Chalet School* was only ever published in paperback with *The Chalet School and Rosalie* but should be numbered 21a in this sequence (see list on pp27–29).

Girls Gone By are following the numbering system of the original hardbacks. All titles will eventually be republished, but not all will be in print at the same time.

Apart from *The Chalet School and Rosalie*, Chambers published four other 'extra' titles: *The Chalet Book for Girls*, *The Second Chalet Book for Girls*, *The Third Chalet Book for Girls* and *The Chalet Girls' Cookbook. The Chalet Book for Girls* included *The Mystery at the Chalet School* as well as three other Chalet School short stories, one non-Chalet story by EBD, and four articles. *The Second Chalet Book for Girls* included the first half of *Tom Tackles the Chalet School*, together with two Chalet School short stories, one other story by EBD, seven articles (including the start of what was to become *The Chalet Girls' Cookbook*) and a rather didactic photographic article called *Beth's Diary*, which featured Beth Chester going to Devon and Cornwall. *The Third Chalet Book for Girls* included the second half of *Tom Tackles the Chalet School* (called *Tom Plays the Game*) as well as two Chalet School short stories, three other stories by EBD and three articles. (Clearly the dustwrapper was printed before the book, since the back flap lists three stories and two articles which are not in the book.) It is likely that *The Chalet School and Rosalie* was intended to be the long story for a fourth *Book for Girls*, but since no more were published this title eventually appeared in 1951 in paperback (very unusual for the time). The back cover of *The Second Chalet Book for Girls* lists *The First Junior Chalet Book* as hopefully being published 'next year'; this never materialised. *The Chalet Girls' Cookbook* is not merely a collection of recipes but also contains a very loose story about Joey, Simone, Marie and Frieda just after they have left the School. While not all of these Chalet stories add crucial information to the series, many of them do, and they are certainly worth collecting. All the *Books for Girls* are difficult to obtain on the second-hand market, but most of the stories were reprinted in two books compiled by Helen McClelland, *Elinor M. Brent-Dyer's Chalet School* and *The Chalet School Companion*, both now out of print but not too difficult to obtain second-hand. Girls Gone By have now published all EBD's known short stories, from these and other sources, in a single volume.

The Locations of the Chalet School Books
The Chalet School started its life in Briesau am Tiernsee in the Austrian Tyrol (Pertisau am Achensee in real life). After Germany signed the Anschluss with Austria in 1938, it would have been impossible to keep even a fictional school in Austria. As a result, EBD wrote *The Chalet School in Exile*, during which, following an encounter with some Nazis, several of the girls, including Joey Bettany, were forced to flee Austria, and the School was also forced to leave. Unfortunately, Elinor chose to move the School to Guernsey—the book was published just as Germany invaded the Channel Islands. The next book, *The Chalet School Goes to It*, saw the School moving again, this time to a village near Armiford—Hereford in real life. Here the School remained for the duration of the war, and indeed when the next move came, in *The Chalet School and the Island*, it was for reasons of plot. The island concerned was off the south-west coast of Wales, and is fictional, although generally agreed by Chalet School fans to be a combination of various islands including Caldey Island, St Margaret's Isle, Skokholm, Ramsey Island and Grassholm, with Caldey Island being the most likely contender if a single island has to be picked. Elinor had long wanted to move the School back to Austria, but the political situation there in the 1950s forbade such a move, so she did the next best thing and moved it to Switzerland, firstly by establishing a finishing branch in *The Chalet School and the Oberland*, and secondly by relocating the School itself in *The Chalet School and Barbara*. The exact location is subject to much debate, but it seems likely that it is

somewhere near Wengen in the Bernese Oberland. Here the School was to remain for the rest of its fictional life, and here it still is today for its many aficionados.

The Chalet Club 1959–69

In 1959 Chambers and Elinor Brent-Dyer started a club for lovers of the Chalet books, beginning with 33 members. When the club closed in 1969, after Elinor's death, there were around 4,000 members worldwide. Twice-yearly News Letters were produced, written by Elinor herself, and the information in these adds fascinating, if sometimes conflicting, detail to the series. In 1997 Friends of the Chalet School, one of the two fan clubs existing today, republished the News Letters in facsimile book format. A new edition is now available from Girls Gone By Publishers.

The Publication of the Chalet School Series in Armada Paperback

On 1 May 1967, Armada, the children's paperback division of what was then William Collins, Sons & Co Ltd, published the first four Chalet School paperbacks. This momentous news was covered in issue Number Sixteen of the Chalet Club News Letter, which also appeared in May 1967. In her editorial, Elinor Brent-Dyer said: 'Prepare for a BIG piece of news. The Chalet Books, slightly abridged, are being reissued in the Armada series. The first four come out in May, and two of them are *The School at the Chalet* and *Jo of the Chalet School*. So watch the windows of the booksellers if you want to add them to your collection. They will be issued at the usual Armada price, which should bring them within the reach of all of you. I hope you like the new jackets. Myself, I think them charming, especially *The School at the Chalet*.' On the back page of the News Letter there was an advertisement for the books, which reproduced the covers of the first four titles.

The words 'slightly abridged' were a huge understatement, and over the years Chalet fans have made frequent complaints about the fact that the paperbacks are abridged, about some of the covers, and about the fact that the books were published in a most extraordinary order, with the whole series never available in paperback at any one time. It has to be said, however, that were it not for the paperbacks interest in the Chalet series would, in the main, be confined to those who had bought or borrowed the hardbacks prior to their demise in the early 1970s, and Chalet fans would mostly be at least 40 and over in age. The paperbacks have sold hundreds of thousands of copies over the years, and those that are not in print (the vast majority) are still to be found on the second-hand market (through charity shops and jumble sales as well as dealers). They may be cut (and sometimes disgracefully so), but enough of the story is there to fascinate new readers, and we should be grateful that they were published at all. Had they not been, it is most unlikely that two Chalet clubs would now be flourishing and that Girls Gone By Publishers would be able to republish the series in this new, unabridged, format.

Clarissa Cridland
2002

ELINOR M BRENT-DYER: A BRIEF BIOGRAPHY

EBD was born Gladys Eleanor May Dyer in South Shields on 6 April 1894, the only daughter of Eleanor (Nelly) Watson Rutherford and Charles Morris Brent Dyer. Her father had been married before and had a son, Charles Arnold, who was never to live with his father and stepmother. This caused some friction between Elinor's parents, and her father left home when she was three and her younger brother, Henzell, was two. Her father eventually went to live with another woman by whom he had a third son, Morris. Elinor's parents lived in a respectable lower-middle-class area, and the family covered up the departure of her father by saying that her mother had 'lost' her husband.

In 1912 Henzell died of cerebro-spinal fever, another event which was covered up. Friends of Elinor's who knew her after his death were unaware that she had had a brother. Death from illness was, of course, common at this time, and Elinor's familiarity with this is reflected in her books, which abound with motherless heroines.

Elinor was educated privately in South Shields, and returned there to teach after she had been to the City of Leeds Training College. In the early 1920s she adopted the name Elinor Mary Brent-Dyer. She was interested in the theatre, and her first book, *Gerry Goes to School*, published in 1922, was written for the child actress Hazel Bainbridge—mother of the actress Kate O'Mara. In the mid 1920s she also taught at St Helen's, Northwood, Middlesex, at Moreton House School, Dunstable, Bedfordshire, and in Fareham near Portsmouth. She was a keen musician and a practising Christian, converting to Roman Catholicism in 1930, a major step in those days.

In the early 1920s Elinor spent a holiday in the Austrian Tyrol at Pertisau am Achensee, which she was to use so successfully as the first location in the Chalet School series. (Many of the locations in her books were real places.) In 1933 she moved with her mother and stepfather to Hereford, travelling daily to Peterchurch as a governess. After her stepfather died in November 1937 she started her own school in Hereford, The Margaret Roper, which ran from 1938 until 1948. Unlike the Chalet School it was not a huge success and probably would not have survived had it not been for the Second World War. From 1948 Elinor devoted all her time to writing. Her mother died in 1957, and in 1964 Elinor moved to Redhill, Surrey, where she died on 20 September 1969.

Clarissa Cridland
2002

COMPLETE NUMERICAL LIST OF TITLES IN THE CHALET SCHOOL SERIES

(Chambers and Girls Gone By)

Dates in parentheses refer to the original publication dates

1. *The School at the Chalet* (1925)
2. *Jo of the Chalet School* (1926)
3. *The Princess of the Chalet School* (1927)
4. *The Head Girl of the Chalet School* (1928)
5. *The Rivals of the Chalet School* (1929)
6. *Eustacia Goes to the Chalet School* (1930)
7. *The Chalet School and Jo* (1931)
8. *The Chalet Girls in Camp* (1932)
9. *The Exploits of the Chalet Girls* (1933)
10. *The Chalet School and the Lintons* (1934) (published in Armada paperback in two volumes—*The Chalet School and the Lintons* and *A Rebel at the Chalet School*)
11. *The New House at the Chalet School* (1935)
12. *Jo Returns to the Chalet School* (1936)
13. *The New Chalet School* (1938) (published in Armada paperback in two volumes—*The New Chalet School* and *A United Chalet School*)
14. *The Chalet School in Exile* (1940)
15. *The Chalet School Goes to It* (1941) (published in Armada paperback as *The Chalet School at War*)
16. *The Highland Twins at the Chalet School* (1942)
17. *Lavender Laughs in the Chalet School* (1943) (published in Armada paperback as *Lavender Leigh at the Chalet School*)
18. *Gay From China at the Chalet School* (1944) (published in Armada paperback as *Gay Lambert at the Chalet School*)
19. *Jo to the Rescue* (1945)

19a. *The Mystery at the Chalet School* (1947) (published in *The Chalet Book for Girls*)

19b. *Tom Tackles the Chalet School* (published in *The Second Chalet Book for Girls*, 1948, and *The Third Chalet Book for Girls*, 1949, and then as a single volume in 1955)

19c. *The Chalet School and Rosalie* (1951) (published as a paperback)

20. *Three Go to the Chalet School* (1949)

21. *The Chalet School and the Island* (1950)

22. *Peggy of the Chalet School* (1950)

23. *Carola Storms the Chalet School* (1951)

24. *The Wrong Chalet School* (1952)

25. *Shocks for the Chalet School* (1952)

26. *The Chalet School in the Oberland* (1952)

27. *Bride Leads the Chalet School* (1953)

28. *Changes for the Chalet School* (1953)

29. *Joey Goes to the Oberland* (1954)

30. *The Chalet School and Barbara* (1954)

31. (see 19b)

32. *The Chalet School Does It Again* (1955)

33. *A Chalet Girl from Kenya* (1955)

34. *Mary-Lou of the Chalet School* (1956)

35. *A Genius at the Chalet School* (1956) (published in Armada paperback in two volumes—*A Genius at the Chalet School* and *Chalet School Fête*)

36. *A Problem for the Chalet School* (1956)

37. *The New Mistress at the Chalet School* (1957)

38. *Excitements at the Chalet School* (1957)

39. *The Coming of Age of the Chalet School* (1958)

40. *The Chalet School and Richenda* (1958)

41. *Trials for the Chalet School* (1958)

42. *Theodora and the Chalet School* (1959)

43. *Joey and Co in Tirol* (1960)

44. *Ruey Richardson—Chaletian* (1960) (published in Armada paperback as *Ruey Richardson at the Chalet School*)
45. *A Leader in the Chalet School* (1961)
46. *The Chalet School Wins the Trick* (1961)
47. *A Future Chalet School Girl* (1962)
48. *The Feud in the Chalet School* (1962)
49. *The Chalet School Triplets* (1963)
50. *The Chalet School Reunion* (1963)
51. *Jane and the Chalet School* (1964)
52. *Redheads at the Chalet School* (1964)
53. *Adrienne and the Chalet School* (1965)
54. *Summer Term at the Chalet School* (1965)
55. *Challenge for the Chalet School* (1966)
56. *Two Sams at the Chalet School* (1967)
57. *Althea Joins the Chalet School* (1969)
58. *Prefects of the Chalet School* (1970)

Extras

The Chalet Book for Girls (1947)
The Second Chalet Book for Girls (1948)
The Third Chalet Book for Girls (1949)
The Chalet Girls' Cookbook (1953)

COMPLETE NUMERICAL LIST OF TITLES IN THE CHALET SCHOOL SERIES

(Armada/Collins)

1.   *The School at the Chalet*
2.   *Jo of the Chalet School*
3.   *The Princess of the Chalet School*
4.   *The Head Girl of the Chalet School*
5.   *(The) Rivals of the Chalet School*
6.   *Eustacia Goes to the Chalet School*
7.   *The Chalet School and Jo*
8.   *The Chalet Girls in Camp*
9.   *The Exploits of the Chalet Girls*
10. *The Chalet School and the Lintons*
11. *A Rebel at the Chalet School*
12. *The New House at the Chalet School*
13. *Jo Returns to the Chalet School*
14. *The New Chalet School*
15. *A United Chalet School*
16. *The Chalet School in Exile*
17. *The Chalet School at War*
18. *The Highland Twins at the Chalet School*
19. *Lavender Leigh at the Chalet School*
20. *Gay Lambert at the Chalet School*
21. *Jo to the Rescue*
21a. *The Mystery at the Chalet School* (published only in the same volume as 23)
22. *Tom Tackles the Chalet School*
23. *The Chalet School and Rosalie*
24. *Three Go to the Chalet School*
25. *The Chalet School and the Island*
26. *Peggy of the Chalet School*

NEW CHALET SCHOOL TITLES

In the last few years several authors have written books which either fill in terms in the Chalet School canon about which Elinor did not write or carry on the story. These are as follows:

Juliet of the Chalet School by Caroline German—set in the gap between *Jo of the Chalet School* and *The Princess of the Chalet School*; it tells of Juliet's debut as Head Girl (Girls Gone By Publishers 2006)

Visitors for the Chalet School by Helen McClelland—set between *The Princess of the Chalet School* and *The Head Girl of the Chalet School* (Bettany Press 1995; Collins edition 2000)

Gillian of the Chalet School by Carol Allan—set between *The New Chalet School* and *The Chalet School in Exile* (Girls Gone By Publishers 2001; reprinted 2006; out of print)

The Chalet School and Robin by Caroline German—set after *The Chalet School Goes to It* (Girls Gone By Publishers 2003; out of print)

A Chalet School Headmistress by Helen Barber—set during the same term as *The Mystery at the Chalet School* (Girls Gone By Publishers 2004; out of print)

Peace Comes to the Chalet School by Katherine Bruce—set in the gap between *The Chalet School and Rosalie* and *Three Go to the Chalet School*; the action takes place during the summer term of 1945 (Girls Gone By Publishers 2005; out of print)

New Beginnings at the Chalet School by Heather Paisley—set three years after *Prefects at the Chalet School* (Friends of the Chalet School 1999; Girls Gone By Publishers 2002; reprinted 2006)

FURTHER READING

Behind the Chalet School by Helen McClelland (essential)*

Elinor M. Brent-Dyer's Chalet School by Helen McClelland. Out of print.

The Chalet School Companion by Helen McClelland. Out of print.

A World of Girls by Rosemary Auchmuty. Out of print.

A World of Women by Rosemary Auchmuty*

*Available from:
Bettany Press, 8 Kildare Road, London E16 4AD, UK
(http://users.netmatters.co.uk/ju90/ordering.htm)

PREFECTS OF THE CHALET SCHOOL

ELINOR M. BRENT-DYER

CONTENTS

To
PHYL
With Love

Chapter I

THE PREFECTS DISCUSS PLANS

"PREFECTS' Meeting already! What's the why of that?" Audrey Everett swung about to cast a look round the half-dozen or so girls who had followed her down Hall to the big notice-board at which she had been staring amazedly.

Eve Hurrell, the Senior Librarian, shrugged her shoulders. "Don't ask me. I haven't a clue. I know we've a fair amount to discuss, but I should have thought we might have waited until to-morrow at least. We arranged a good deal during the earlier meetings, didn't we? The main part of the Sale anyhow. Apart from details I should have said we fixed all that as far as possible. What else have we to deal with?"

"There's the Sports, of course. Oh, I know we began on various heats the week before last, but we've some sort of programme to draw up, I suppose," Carmela Walther remarked, tugging at one of the curly tendrils that had escaped from the black velvet band round her head.

"I thought Burney and that crowd saw to that," Priscilla Dawbarn said.

"They always did; but do you not remember that during last Christmas term it was decided that we should do it ourselves this year?" It was Marie Huber, the Music prefect, who spoke.

"Well, we can't do anything about it until we have consulted with the Games staff," Carmela said. "But we ought to go upstairs, I think." She glanced at her watch. "We must be in the Speisesaal on duty at 18.30 and it is now 18.10."

"And besides, here come two more of the coaches, so let us

go and tidy," proposed Maria Zinkel, a Swiss girl who looked as if she had stepped from a bandbox already.

Eve laughed. "Yes! You need it so badly, Maria! How you do it is more than I can say. Are you *never* untidy?"

"Oh, but often! Have you forgotten the day I upset the flour in Dommy Sci and emerged with white hair instead of black?" Maria asked with a demure twinkle.

The prefects broke into a chorus of laughter as they followed Carmela out of Hall, turned into the wide entrance hall and ran gaily up the stately staircase leading to the upper floors, just as sundry mistresses appeared from the corridor and passages which ran back from the entrance hall to the classrooms forming the main part of the building. At the same time the great doors were flung open and the first coach delivered up its load of jolly, laughing Middles.

At the head of the stairs stood a small, wiry woman in the crisp uniform of a school matron. The girls clustered round her with greetings and she put up her hands to ward them off while she gave them a smiling welcome.

"Steady, you giants! Remember to hit one of your own size. Yes; I am aware that the bulk of the school is on us and you had better go and deposit your cases and then come down prepared for duty."

"Did you have a good holiday?" Priscilla asked as she turned to go down the corridor towards her own quarters.

"Very pleasant, thank you, and a real rest. Now be off, all of you!"

They scattered at once. When Matey, as the school at large called her, gave an order, even the mistresses obeyed. She was, to quote Mrs Maynard, mother of Len and her triplet sisters Con and Margot, one of the foundation stones of the school. Apart from that, though she was little she was a martinet and always had been.

Matron herself descended the wide, shallow stairs and reached the entrance hall just as the buses were discharging their loads. Miss Annersley, the Head, was waiting to welcome her pupils, and those members of staff who had already arrived were joining her.

"What a nuisance the rain is," Miss Lawrence, head of the Music staff, remarked to Miss Wilmot, who had just joined her on the stairs.

"Well, at least we've had fine weather for the half-term," Miss Wilmot rejoined. "Had a good time, Dorothy?"

"Excellent, thank you. What about you?"

"Ah-*ha*! You wait until we're free and I'll unfold a tale second to none." Miss Wilmot's blue eyes were dancing. "Here they come! Stand by to repel boarders!" For at this point the first of the girls were marching in to take up their places according to forms and the mistresses all stopped talking and turned to face the throng and respond to their greetings.

The prefects were hurrying to take up their posts among the younger girls, having come down by the back staircases, and Len Maynard, as Head Girl, was hurriedly scanning the long lines to make sure that they were in order.

Miss Annersley beamed on the crowd when the last of the girls was standing in her place.

"Welcome back, girls. I hope you've had a happy time this weekend."

A chorus assured her of that. She nodded and continued, "And I hope you've all come back prepared to do your best with what is left of the term. We shall be very busy, as I expect you know. We have our Regatta at the end of the month. Then there are the Sports and finally, and most important, our Annual Sale. I say nothing of the exams," she added laughing, "but I'm hoping that this year will be a record year where they are concerned. Now the rest of what I have to say to you may wait, for I know Karen and Co have Abendessen waiting and I am sure you are all ready for it. So you may march to the Splasheries and tidy yourselves, and then to the Speisesaal."

She looked across the sea of heads towards Miss Lawrence, who was now seated at the grand piano, and gave her a signal. The mistress swung round on the music stool and crashed into a favourite march as the girls turned and, led by the Juniors, marched off to the Splasheries, to hang up raincoats and caps, change into house shoes and, after tidying their hair, line up again to promenade quietly to the long, narrow room known to them as the Speisesaal.

Here, they took places behind their seats. The staff appeared at the high table and, after grace had been said, they sat down. A buzz of quiet chatter filled the room while they settled down to slices of home-made brawn accompanied by hunches of crusty bread smothered with butter. This was followed by dishes of wild strawberries heaped with a creamy pink mixture for which Karen, head of the kitchen staff, was renowned.

That finished, grace was said, and while the elder girls set to work to clear the tables, those of the prefects not already busy overseeing this went off upstairs to give an eye to the unpacking of weekend cases in the dormitories. This done, the girls went downstairs again, and the prefects hurried off to their room.

Len was in her seat at the head of the table, Ted Grantley, the second prefect, on her right hand, and her sister Margot, the Games prefect, on her left.

Seated at the foot was Con Maynard, the editor of the school magazine, the *Chaletian*, a slim dark girl who wore her thick black hair in plaited shells over her ears. Margot's red-gold curls were cropped, and Len's chestnut mane was tightly plaited and coiled low on the nape of her neck. The other prefects varied from this to Ted Grantley's straight black crop brushed back over her head in a boyish cut.

Apart from that they were trim in the school's summer uniform of plain cotton frocks with embroidered collars and cuffs. For the most part they were pleasant-looking girls with an air of capability about them.

When Jeanne Daudet, the prefect responsible for attendance on the staff, had taken her seat, they turned expectant looks on Len, and she got to her feet.

"Well, everyone, we haven't a lot of time, for we must get down to business," she said. "We've got to arrange the programme for the Sports first of all. Also the Regatta. This will be the first proper Regatta we've held since we left the Island, and we had the place more or less to ourselves then."

"What fun it was," Primrose said wistfully. "And do you remember our water pageant?"

Len chuckled. "Do I not! And how Tom as *Triton* blew on her conch-shell and nearly scared the horse Peggy and Dickie were riding into bolting."

"We can't hope for any excitement of that kind nowadays." Priscilla heaved a deep sigh.

Margot chuckled. "I've always been sorry we three missed that show. We were in Canada at the time. It was a good time, but I *would* have liked to see that pageant. Oh, well, you can't have everything."

"You certainly can't," Con said briskly, "and there's no question of a water pageant this year, so let's get down to what we *are* going to have. Margot, has anything been arranged?"

"Pretty well everything," Margot replied. "The only thing we have to fix is what oddments we are going to have besides the swimming and rowing races and the diving. Anyone got any ideas?"

"I think we ought to have the tub races. They are always good fun," Eve said.

"Where are we getting the tubs?" Ted demanded. "There aren't

41

any in the laundry nowadays that I know of—only washing machines. We could hardly use those."

"Oh goodness!" It came in a chorus. "What can we do about that?"

It was a tricky question. "Could we not borrow from the people on the Platz?" Marie asked.

"We might, I suppose," Len said doubtfully. "It will be difficult, and how do we get the said tubs down to the lake?"

"Take them down in one of the coaches," Ted suggested.

"I suppose we could," Margot said.

"We'd better discuss it with Burney," Len said. "We'll have to leave it in abeyance for the moment at any rate. Well, is everyone agreed to that? Yes? Then there isn't anything more to do there. We have to fix the life-saving classes and that will finish that. Who's running them?"

"Me," said Audrey. "You're giving me a hand there, aren't you, Carmela? We could do with a couple more, Len."

"I'll give you a hand," Marie offered.

"Oh, good! Anyone else? What about you, Primrose? You're pretty good at it, aren't you?"

Primrose made a face. "Must I? I'm up to the eyes in the long jump and high jump, for the Sports. We've hardly done a thing about the heats for them as yet. Can't you get someone else to do it?"

"What about you, Ruey?" Margot glanced at Ruey Richardson. "You haven't anything special yet, have you?"

Ruey, a brown-eyed girl with trim brown hair framing a thin freckled face, shook her head. "Not *yet*!" she said with deep meaning in her voice.

"Well, what about it?" Len asked.

"I'll do it if you want me to and there's no one else."

"Then we'll leave it at that. Is that everything settled, Margot? I don't know what we can do about the fancy races; I very much doubt if we can manage the tub races—well, Joan? Got an idea for us?"

"Yes—what about porpoise races?"

"Good for you!" Margot exclaimed. "I'd forgotten about them and they're always good fun. What's more, they're tied down to the Seniors, so we don't have to worry about heats for the kids. Anyone anything to say on the subject?" She glanced round the table.

Everyone agreed enthusiastically. Porpoise races were fun, not only for the competitors, but for the onlookers. It was decided to consult Miss Burnett, the Games mistress, and, subject to her assent, to run off inter-form races.

"Now is that everything?" Len demanded.

"I should imagine so," Con said. "We've fixed up most of the Sale, haven't we? Then we'd better see what we can do about the Sports. What's left to settle apart from the usuals?"

A tap on the door interrupted the discussion.

"Come in, whoever you are," Margot sang out. The door opened to admit three members of the Senior Middles who sidled in looking rather overcome, but determined nevertheless.

Len stared at them. "Erica—Althea—Jocelyn—what on earth do you want?" she demanded.

"You're having a meeting about the Sports, aren't you?" Erica asked.

"We are; but what business it is of yours at the moment I don't see," Len told her. "The notices will be going up at the end of the week and we're not going to confide in you folk until then."

"Oh, that isn't what we wanted to say," Erica said reddening.

"Well, what is it then? Be quick for we haven't much time left and we want to get this part of it finished before Prayers."

The three looked at each other. Finally Jocelyn, a thirteen-year-old, found her voice. "Please, we wondered if we could hire

43

some motor-boats, and have, say, three motor-boat races?" she blurted out.

The prefects gazed at her, almost bereft of their breath at this suggestion. Margot was the first to recover herself.

"What on earth put such a mad idea into your heads? Of course we couldn't. In the first place none of us has had enough experience in handling the things even if we had any to practise with. In the second where do you imagine we could hire them? In the third—do you really think anyone would agree to such a thing—especially after the doing we had from *one* motor-boat the other week?"

Jocelyn was not prepared to give up so readily. "It would be so awfully with it, to have a thing like that," she urged.

"I daresay," Margot said sceptically, "but I'm afraid you'll find that the Head and Burney and everyone else concerned on the staff will prefer that we let that sort of thing alone. We like our Sports, aquatic or dry-land, to be on the safe side. If you think anyone, ourselves, staff or parents, would consent to anything so uncertain, that's where your toes turn in."

"But it needn't be unsafe any more than rowing," Erica pleaded.

Ted grinned. "Have you forgotten that you'd have to have drivers' licences?"

"Not car licences, surely?" Jocelyn countered. "Surely boats are different. And it would be so—so nifty."

"Nifty or not," Len retorted, "we're not having it—not this year, at any rate. So scram, the lot of you. You're wasting our time—and yours, too, if it comes to that. The answer is 'no' every time, so don't come bothering us again, please. Off you go!"

There was a silence, then Erica turned to the door and her two partners turned reluctantly to follow her. But they were not prepared to give up what had struck them as a really original idea for the Regatta. As they reached the door Jocelyn stopped and turned.

"You're not the only people to decide on what sports we shall have," she said cheekily. "If you won't agree, we'll go to Burney. She's a lot of a sport and it's just possible she may decide that ours is a jolly good idea and worth trying out."

But this was too much. Len stood up. "That will do. Impudence to the prefects won't get you anywhere, Jocelyn. Take yourselves off and be thankful that this is the last day of half-term. *Off!*"

Under the stern looks from the prefects even Jocelyn was not prepared to argue any more just then; but if Len and Co thought they had settled the matter in short order they were to find out their mistake. And so they learned before they were much older.

Chapter II

MOTOR-BOATS

"WHAT I'd like to know is who started those demons off on that idea?" Margot looked round her fellow prefects with gleaming eyes. Prayers were over, and all of the school up to and including Upper IVa had retired to bed. The Seniors had another hour's grace and most of the girls were making the most of it in Hall where they were dancing gaily. Only the three Maynards, with Ted, Carmela, Audrey and Ruey were sitting in a group at the far end of Hall, discussing the Senior Middles' latest.

"Jocelyn, for a ducat," Len answered her sister. "It's just the mad sort of thing she would think of. As for the other two, Erica has been growing matier with her; and Althea, I happen to know, is crackers on boats of any and every kind, though I must say I didn't think she'd pal up with a demon like Jocelyn."

"You never know, do you?" Con observed. "It's no use looking worried over that connection, Len. We can't butt in on their friendship, my love. They'd resent it furiously and I shouldn't blame them. We'd have raged if they'd tried to do it with us and well you know it."

"Oh, I know that. You don't have to tell me," Len agreed. "At the same time I don't like it. Jocelyn may have improved somewhat since her first days here, but she's no model and she does have a most unholy influence on her own crowd."

"We can't help that," Ted pointed out.

"No; but if we don't keep an eye on her, we're going to lay up lots of trouble for ourselves," Con pointed out. "You know what Mamma has always said—that it's better to be safe than sorry.

Where that crew are concerned I couldn't agree more. Only I don't quite see what we are to do about it."

"My own suggestion is to keep them so hard at it that they haven't time to dream up mad ideas," Ruey observed.

"Well—such as how?" Margot queried.

Len laughed. "Margot! What ghastly English! If the Abbess heard you she'd have a fit!"

"You leave my English alone and see if you can't think of anything to occupy those imps and keep them off motor-boats."

"But that's just what I can't do at the moment," Len complained.

Audrey raised her eyebrows. "Do you honestly think they're likely to play round with the idea? I should have said there were too many obstacles in the way for them to do that. First they'd have to get leave from the Head. Then they'd have to provide their boats. I should have said that would be enough to be going on with."

"Where Erica and Althea are concerned I'd have agreed with you, but Jocelyn is another pair of shoes. To start with she seems to do whatever comes into her head without bothering to consider consequences. Look how she went off last Christmas Term and nearly did Mary-Lou and herself in as a result."

"She has tried to do better since then," Con pointed out to Margot whose remark this last was. "In spots, anyhow," she amended her comment.

"It's a pity they don't come oftener," Ted said feelingly.

Len sighed. "This is the last of our schooldays proper and I did hope they'd be normally peaceful, but if Jocelyn and Co have got their tails up it isn't likely to come off—not if I know anything of that crowd. But I'm sorry Erica and Althea look like being mixed up in it."

"Who else do you think would join in?" Audrey asked.

"Hard to say. Astrid Andersen—Rita Quick—Carlotta

von Eschenau—Maureen O'Toole—Sandra Johnson—all that lot."

"Not Carlotta," Con said quickly, "I wouldn't bet on any of the others, but Carlotta isn't too mad on water sports. I should think she'll fight anything like that."

"Well, I suppose that's something to be thankful for," Margot remarked. "But what surprises me more than the rest is the way Jocelyn cheeked us over it. What's taken the silly little ass?"

"Your guess is as good as mine. And if you hoped for a peaceful period, Len, you did have a hope! You ought to know by this time that the Chalet School has never yet been famous for producing a gaggle of baby angels among its Middles. We weren't such models ourselves when we were at that age. I suppose all we can do is to hope for the best and prepare for the worst."

As the bell for their bedtime sounded just then, they had to leave it at that, but some of the more thoughtful of them finally went off with an uneasy feeling that this second half of the summer term looked like being a term of worry for them.

Meanwhile, the Middles had retired to bed indignant that their wonderful idea had been so flatly and instantly crushed by the prefects. Erica and Althea were nearly as furious about it as Jocelyn, though neither would have gone as far as the latter in making their resentment known and, to tell the truth, both had been more than a little startled by their leader's daring. But they themselves had agreed with her and neither had any idea of drawing back now. As they were all in different houses, not to speak of different dormitories, they were unable to discuss the matter any further that night; but Jocelyn contrived to arrange with both to meet in the grounds next morning before Frühstück, as the school called breakfast, and see what they could do about it.

"If it's fine," Althea stipulated. "If it's wet you know what Matey would say if she caught us. There's no point in starting a row with her until we must."

Jocelyn might have objected furiously to this, but Erica heartily agreed with Althea and there was nothing to be said for going by herself just yet.

"O.K." she said reluctantly, "but let's hope it's a fine day." After that they parted and went to bed where, despite their agitated feelings, they fell asleep almost at once. After all, they had had a fairly full day.

The next day turned out to be fine, the rain having blown over during the night. Unless one had music practice before Frühstück, a run in the garden was permissible first thing in the morning. The School believed in plenty of fresh air for its pupils. Many of the girls had relatives who were up on the Platz for the sake of their health and the staff of both the Sanatorium and the School set health above most things. The wicked trio were easily able to slip off to a secret place in the garden where they could discuss their plans in private.

"Well? What are we going to do about it?" Jocelyn demanded when she and her fellow-criminals were safely hidden.

"*Can* we do anything?" Erica asked.

"I should hope so!" Jocelyn retorted. "I don't know about you, but I'm not going to sit down under snubbing like that and so I warn you."

Althea considered. "Come to that, I expect the prees felt they weren't going to sit down under cheek of the kind you gave them yesterday evening," she said slowly. "I know it was maddening to have your idea cut at like that; all the same, you did cheek them for all you were worth, Jos. They wouldn't be up to much as prees if they took it lying down."

Jocelyn flushed. "I didn't mean it for sauce—not in the beginning. It wasn't until they began that it happened. Then I felt so mad with them. Anyhow it's done now and I for one won't back out."

Erica grinned. "You don't have to tell us that, my love."

Jocelyn looked at her from under knitted brows. "What do you mean?"

"What I say. Oh, come off it, Jos! We all know that once you start going baldheaded at a thing, you stick to it and hang the consequences!"

Jocelyn flushed. "What else do you expect me to do? But you don't have to join in if you funk it," she added.

"I'm not funking it. I'm just pointing out that it won't be easy to manage it!" retorted Erica. "To start with, where are we going to get the boats?"

"Hire them. There are lots of places round the lake where they hire out motor-boats."

"I know that, but how are we getting round to them?"

"We'll have to think it out, of course. That won't be so frightfully hard."

"Where are we keeping them, supposing we do manage to get hold of them?" Althea asked.

"Oh, I've thought of that. We'll have to rent a boat-house."

Erica looked at her meditatively. "Yes; where's the cash for all this hiring coming from?"

"Pocket-money—and bank. I've got a fair amount because I spent the half-term with my aunt, and uncle paid for everything. I'm willing to give all that towards expenses."

"Your aunt? I thought she refused to have anything to do with you?" Erica exclaimed.

"Oh, not *that* aunt. This is my mother's youngest sister and her husband. They come from America and Uncle Jefferson has piles of money and we'd never met before and he said he wanted to make it a boomer of a hol—vacation, he called it—for me. So he did. You wait till I show you what he and Aunt Vinnie gave me while I was with them! She's quite young, you know—not much older than Len Maynard and he's dead nuts on her and so's she on him."

Althea screwed up her nose. "What a horrid thing to say!"

Jocelyn reddened. "Oh, well; that's what he said. Anyhow, what does it matter? There's no kids around to pick up new slang."

"O.K.," Erica said. "But just you be careful not to use it when there are. I'm jolly sure it would be banned if any of the prees or staff heard you use it."

So was Jocelyn—very sure. She changed the subject hurriedly. "This isn't getting on with our plans. I honestly don't think we'll have much trouble about the boats. What is bothering me is how we're to put in any practice."

"We can't," said Althea flatly. "It's a gaudy idea, Jos, but I simply don't see how we're to work it unless we can get the prees to take it up. I thought that was the idea. We can't possibly hope to do it off our own bats and you know it. *My* idea is to canvass among our own crowd for people who will vote for it and get as many as we can and then go to the prees with their votes. If we could get enough there might be just a chance they would give in about it. But we haven't a hope of doing it on our own."

Even Jocelyn saw that. She had had some thought of making a Middles affair of it, but she had quickly given that up. She heaved a sigh.

"No; I suppose we can't though it would have been nifty if we could. However I quite see that we can't. Then we must concentrate on canvassing for votes from everyone we can. Now, how should we begin?"

Erica gave a chuckle. "Well, leave the prees out of it, anyway. We'd better get down to our own crowd. We can attend to that at once."

"Would you leave all the Seniors out?" Althea asked.

"Rather not! I'll tell you who would be with us all right— Jack Lambert. And if Jack would come in, we'd probably get most of her crowd as well. You know that she's crackers on motors and things," Erica said.

"That's true enough. I wonder if she would?" Jocelyn mused.

"She might if we put it to her carefully," Erica replied.

"What do you mean—'carefully'?" Jocelyn demanded.

"Well, don't say anything about last night, for one thing," Althea said.

"No reason why we should. It's a good idea; and how are we—er—to break the news to them? They are Seniors, remember. They might very well sniff at it just because it's our idea and we're only Middles," Erica pointed out.

For once, Jocelyn agreed to be cautious. "We'd better tackle our own lot first and get as many as we can to go for it. Then we can tell them that we aren't the only ones. And I'll tell you what. We could ask them to do the proposing part of it. Only we'll have to buck up about it. There isn't a lot of time and we've got to work it up as hard as we can."

Further than this they could not go at the moment and as the gardens and tennis courts were beginning to fill up they decided to give it a rest and went out from their hidey-hole in the shrubbery to join the others in activities that were lawful.

Erica went off to practise volleying with Samantha van der Byl, an American girl in Inter V; the other two who were entered for the long jump raced off to join a select sextette who were hard at work on the playing field. On their way they passed the three Maynards who were heading for the area where a bunch of Juniors were hard at work on running practice, and in much need of a little guidance in the art of sprinting.

"There they go!" Margot said. "Let's hope last night's do was a mere temporary insanity."

"More than probably," Len said as she waved her hand to the three in passing. She laughed. "It was an enterprising effort, but I'm afraid we couldn't encourage it."

"Hardly," Con agreed. "Anyhow, I, for one, had enough of motor-boats the first half of the term."

"So, I imagine, had Ferry. I shall never know how she managed to stop that crew in time. I still feel sick when I think of it," Len shuddered.

"Oh, well, you don't have to worry about it at the Sports," Margot said cheerfully. "Heavens above! Look at the style of those kids! No one would ever think they'd been taught a thing about running. En avant, mes amies! This is where we begin work!"

Chapter III

Jack Becomes Responsible

Jack Lambert, a bright and shining light of Inter V, was hurrying round to the garage yard behind the school to spend a free half-hour in work on the little car which was owned by three of the mistresses. It was her greatest delight, for Jack, although nearing her sixteenth year, was far more of a boy than a girl. She revelled in all machinery, especially motors. She had been encouraged in the taste by a father who was equally keen. His only son not being more than ordinarily interested he had turned to his younger daughter for sympathy.

When certain members of the staff had discovered in which direction her tastes lay, they had done what they could to provide a little satisfaction for her, and as she and she only had the run of the garages and tools, Jack kept the privilege jealously to herself. No one else had shown any special desire to share it so far, though Jocelyn Marvell eyed her enviously at intervals, being more or less the same type of girl, though so far neither knew it. Jack was not given to mixing much with her juniors and even Jocelyn the cheeky rather shied at treating the senior to her usual hail-fellow-well-met manner. Jack had a short way with her on occasion.

At this moment, however, Jocelyn had a definite end in view and she pulled up as she reached Jack and said, "I say, Jack, can I speak to you?"

Jack glanced at her watch. "Well, hurry up about it. I haven't any too much time."

"Well, could I speak to you later then? It—it's really important."

Jack stared. "What on earth do you want? If it's to do some sports coaching," she added, "I'm sorry, but I haven't any time till this evening. I've got a job on now which will take me every spare moment, and then I've a lesson at 15.00 hours."

This was not encouraging, but Jocelyn was nothing if not persistent. What was more she was none too sure that Erica and Althea were likely to go on backing her up if the prefects continued in their present attitude. If she could get Jack to take up the idea for her there would be more hope for her, she thought.

"It's not sports coaching, it's just—I want to ask you about an idea I've got for the Sports, though."

"Then it'll have to wait. But why don't you take it to Margot or one of the prees?"

Jocelyn had expected this and was ready for it. "It's—I'd like to talk it over with someone like you first," she said.

"Good luck! I hope you don't expect much in the way of words of wisdom from me," Jack ejaculated. "Very well. Meet me at the top of the steps to the rock garden after Kaffee und Kuchen and I'll give you ten minutes then. But it won't be more than ten minutes," she added warningly, "and I still think you'd do better to apply to a pree. However, if that will do you, I'll manage it somehow."

Jocelyn thanked her and then went off to her own quarters to make the best of it. It was hardly encouraging, but she guessed it was all she was likely to get just then, and teasing would get her nowhere. As for Jack, she rushed on to the garage yard feeling rather stunned. She would have refused out of hand, but a sudden memory of the way she herself had tackled Len Maynard during her own earlier days at school, and the way Len had answered her questions and helped her on numerous occasions came in time to prevent it. During the past term or two Len had put her off by insisting that she must try to find her own answers when possible, but Jack knew that if it came to a real crisis she would find help if she really needed it. In all common decency she could hardly refuse to listen to Jocelyn, even if that young woman's wants proved to be beyond her.

"But what possessed her to pitch on *me* as a Mentor," thought Jack with a sudden recollection of her last literature lesson, "is beyond me!"

She gave up any further thought on the subject and became immersed in her own affairs.

Meanwhile the prefects were also much too occupied with their own interests to think a second time about what struck them as one of the maddest suggestions they had ever heard. What school was likely to provide motor-boats for the pupils' sports? None that any of them knew.

Len voiced the general opinion when she said the previous evening when they were tidying up, "I'm not going to bother my head about young Jocelyn's latest. I wonder what she's been reading during the hols? Eve, what about giving an eye to that sort of thing?"

"What about doing it yourself?" was Eve's retort.

"Oh, no, my love; you're school librarian. I've quite enough on my plate—without adding to it any more than I need."

"And anyhow who's to say it's their reading?" Ted butted in. "It may quite well be the result of television or the cinema. But I agree with you that it's unnecessary to run round after them over that. It was someone's sudden inspiration and of course it would appeal to girls like Jocelyn. They haven't taken time to think it out. When they do they'll see for themselves how utterly impossible it is. After all they've all got the rudiments of common sense, though I'll admit the majority of 'em don't use it very much."

By the next morning they had more or less forgotten it. Most of VIa were free of examinations this term, but VIb were not so lucky and the three Fifths were up to the eyes in tests of one kind and another. As for the rest of the school, they had end-of-the-term exams to think about, so during school hours they had plenty to occupy their minds. In fact, what with one thing and another, no one had time to spare to look after the exploits of sundry woolly-headed Middles and for once in her life Jocelyn kept in the background; Erica and Althea were not girls who were likely to bring themselves into public notice for no reason whatever.

The day passed quietly and after Kaffee und Kuchen Jocelyn finally headed for the top of the steps leading down to the rock garden, feeling hopeful about Jack.

Jack herself nearly forgot about the appointment, thanks to an encounter with Matron on the subject of her stocking drawer. Matron had spent the early part of the day in a dormitories inspection and had made the pleasing discovery that Miss Jack, who was far from being a tidy mortal, had paired off her stockings with a complete disregard of colours. Matron sent for her and read her a lecture she had never bettered. What was worse, she decreed a stockings inspection before Frühstück next morning for everyone and Jack's own crowd did not hesitate to tell her what they thought of her for bringing that trial on them. At least ten per cent of them had to give up sports and games practice and spend the precious minutes on stockings. What with Matron's strictures and the frankly voiced comments of her contemporaries, Jack was in none too good a humour when her own great friend, Jane Carew, kindly reminded her that she had promised to see Jocelyn Marvell after Kaffee und Kuchen.

"Oh, *blow*!" Jack said crossly. "What does the silly little ass want with me, anyhow? Thanks for reminding me, Jane, for I'd clean forgotten about it. But I wish she'd tackled someone else if she wants advice. Who am I to advise anyone?"

"I couldn't agree with you more," Judy Willoughby said with a giggle.

Val Gardiner grinned as she said with a toss of her red head, "You're only getting back what you've given Len Maynard from the word 'Go'."

"Think I don't know that?" Jack snapped.

"But it may be just a sudden spurt," Flavia Ansell suggested. "You've kept on at Len all the time. And I must say I think she's been angelically patient with you."

"I know that!" This was almost a snarl. "I can jolly well tell you if it weren't for that, young Jocelyn could whistle for my attention. Oh, well, I suppose I'll have to give ten minutes now, but I hope this is the *last* time any of these brats wants advice from me. I'm not a prefect and I don't want to take on a prefect's jobs until and unless I must." And she stalked off to keep her appointment in none too sweet a mood.

Jocelyn was watching for her with some impatience, but when Jack appeared at the top of the steps, she felt a sudden nervousness. She fought it down and came forward.

"I say, it's awfully good of you," she said.

Jack relaxed a little. "Nonsense! It's more or less what one expects of Seniors in this establishment as you ought to know by this time. Now we can't dilly-dally, so let's get down to brass tacks. What's the problem, Jocelyn?"

Jocelyn fidgeted with her fingers. But Jack was waiting, so she pulled herself together and came out with it. "It's just—some of us got an idea for a new race for the Regatta and we thought we'd like to ask someone before we hand it out to Burney," she blurted out.

Jack raised her eyebrows. "What on earth—What's the matter with not telling her straight away? It'll have to go to her, you know. She's the one who makes the final decisions."

"I know; but—but—"

"Well, then?"

"It's—someone thinks it's mad."

"Someone—who?"

"Oh—just someone. The thing is will you listen to it and tell me what *you* think of it?"

Jack looked at her with knitted brows. "But if you've been at someone about it already why do you want to ask me?"

"Because she—they didn't give any time to it. I thought you might think it over first before you said anything. She didn't."

Jack could make nothing of this, but she said resignedly, "Well, go ahead. I'll listen and I'll think it over; but I can't promise you more just now. Here; the arbour is empty, we'll go there. Now sit down and tell me what this is in aid of."

"Well," said Jocelyn as they sat down in the little creeper-covered arbour at the far end of the garden, "it's just—we wondered if we could hire motor-boats and—and have a motor-boat race." Then she sat back and eyed Jack apprehensively.

That young woman was almost literally robbed of breath at the proposal.

"What on earth put that idea into your head?" she demanded finally.

"I don't know actually. I just thought of it—and so did the others."

"What others?"

"Well, it began with me—and Erica and Althea—but we've proposed it to two or three others of our crowd and we're all keen. Oh, Jack, don't you think it would be a good notion? And something quite new."

Jack looked at her thoughtfully. "It's all that. The only thing is I don't see how it could be managed."

"But why not?"

Jack smothered a sigh and faced up to the fact that this was not something that could be settled in a hurry. "Well, for one thing, where's the cash coming from to pay for it?"

"We'd subscribe. And couldn't we call on the Games Funds?"

"Not very likely this year, at any rate. What put you on to it, anyhow?"

"I—well, it just came into my head."

"I see. But, you know, you're on the late side in proposing it, aren't you?"

"Need that make much difference? I—I mean, we'd just have to see about hiring the boats, wouldn't we?"

"You haven't thought it out properly," Jack said. "It means a lot more than that. For one thing, what about practising?"

"I know. But we'd all start together with that, wouldn't we?"

"That's true; but when would the heats be run off?"

"I thought perhaps they might be dodged in when we were down for swimming and rowing."

"Not a hope of that! My good girl, our time is filled up to the last moment. And another thing, so is the mistresses' time. Honestly, Jocelyn, I don't see how it could possibly be done—or not this year."

Jocelyn's face fell. She had never given a thought to all this. "Then—then you won't back us up? Oh, Jack, I thought you would understand."

"So I do. If you'd proposed it last term we might have done something about it and I'd have backed you up all right then, everything else being equal. As it is I don't see how we could do a thing about it now. But," she added hastily, "everything else *isn't* equal. Even if we could get over all those snags, there are others. For instance, who would coach us? And make no mistake, it would mean coaching. No one is going to allow girls to mess about with motor-boats unless there's an expert on the job."

"I—I thought perhaps Ferry could do it. Look what she did with that one last half-term."

"I don't suppose for a moment she could fit it in. I should say myself her time is as full as it will hold."

"She's got lots of the evenings when she doesn't teach or anything."

"Yes; and when do you think she can get a little time to herself? Or didn't you think of that?"

"It wouldn't hurt her to give us an hour or two during the week," muttered Jocelyn.

"Wouldn't it?" said Jack, startling herself by this sudden feeling of sympathy with a mistress. "Now just you think a moment. She teaches cricket on two evenings in the week and tennis on one. She has prep with your lot on another. That's four evenings filled up with odd jobs until Prayers. That leaves her *one* for free time to see to her mending and—and correcting and preparing for her lessons and—and writing letters and going for walks and—well—everything like that. How's she going to fit all that lot in? And after all, why *should* she?"

"She's paid for it, I suppose."

"Oh, no, she isn't!" Jack retorted. "If you'd tried that sort of game on with miners or—or men in factories or shops, or railwaymen—or any kind of worker, you'd find yourself with a lot of strikes on your hands. I know our staff are always ready to lend the odd hand, but you can't expect them to do it as an understood thing. You wouldn't do it yourself."

Jocelyn had nothing to say. She had never thought of anything like that. It is safe to say that neither had Jack for that matter. In fact that young person was surprising herself quite as much as she was surprising her junior by all these details and, as Len Maynard said later, she was growing up in a big burst. Until Jocelyn had appealed to her like this she had taken things very much for granted.

She got up now. "Well, I'd love to back you up and if you like to suggest it for next year's Regatta, I *will* back you up; but it's nothing doing now. You'll have to give it up for the present and wait till next year."

"But I don't *want* to wait," Jocelyn wailed. "Next year may never come!"

Jack was losing patience. "Oh, talk sense! Of course it'll come. I'll have to go now. I'm due elsewhere and I've given you every minute I can. Take my advice, Jocelyn. Shelve it for the moment. *And DIG IN on the races we have this year.* What are you in for?"

Jocelyn mentioned the names of the three races for which she had entered and Jack nodded. "O.K.; you give all you've got for them and wait till next year."

There was no more to be said. Jack had a reputation for meaning what she said and sticking to it. Jocelyn was bitterly disappointed, but she could see that all she could plead was likely to get her nowhere. She mumbled out thanks, but she finally parted with the Senior with a feeling that no one understood. As for all that rot about Ferry's free time well, it *was* rot. She was paid for her work during the term and Jocelyn was far too much of a child to realize that that ought not to include overtime.

"Well?" Althea demanded when she and the other two foregathered later.

"No use," Jocelyn snarled. "Jack's as dumb as the rest of them. She won't help us out. Talked a lot of bilge about mistresses having no time for coaching and all that."

"Then what are we going to do?" asked Erica.

"If we do what they all want we'll give it up. But that's not me! I'll fix it somehow."

"I don't see how," Erica said thoughtfully. "Anyhow, I do agree that we haven't allowed for the timetable. We'll just have to give it up this year and hope for the best for next year."

"That's up to you. Drop out of it if that's what you feel like. What about you, Althea? Are you backing down, too?"

"'Fraid there's no help for it. I'll back you up if you propose it next year, but there's too many snags for this."

"O.K. Have it your own way. I'll go it on my own, so now you know!" And with this Jocelyn stalked off, her nose in the air, her mind more set than ever on getting her own way, never mind who said what!

Chapter IV

ENTER JOEY

BY the Thursday morning of that week, work at the Chalet School was in full swing. Mornings were devoted to lessons. The afternoons were largely given over to art and needlework; sports and games practices; and such extras as singing, Spanish, Italian and Russian, together with preparation periods for the Juniors and Middles. With all this to fill in their time, no one had much to spare for extraneous squabbles. Jocelyn by no means forgot her grievance against the prefects, but those superior young persons thought little more about it. As for Erica and Althea, they easily resigned themselves to giving up the idea for the present. Althea indeed, who had rather more common sense than the other two, nearly caused a breach in their trio by pointing out that there was a lot to be said for turning down the proposition this summer on the score of lack of time.

"After all, the Regatta is supposed to come off at the end of this month," she pointed out. "You can't be surprised that they don't think it could be done."

If it had been a question of only Althea, the whole affair would have ended there, she being more or less law-abiding. Jocelyn was made of sterner stuff. Having determined to hold on to their first idea, she stuck to it, and her influence over Erica was great enough to persuade the young lady to follow her.

Needless to say, the staff heard rumours about what was going on among the Middles and commented on it in the privacy of their own quarters. Peggy Burnett, as Head of the games, had something to say about the cheek of trying to start up anything of the kind without first consulting herself and the mistress who was responsible for physical training in the school, never to speak of the prefects. Her colleagues agreed with her, though after a conference in private Kathy Ferrars, Sharlie Andrews, Rosalind Moore and Nancy Wilmot decided that a firm eye must be kept on the firebrands, though nothing yet was to be said to the Heads.

"They've enough on their plates just now," Kathy pointed out.

"I couldn't agree more, but I see no reason why we shouldn't consult Joey Maynard," Miss Burnett announced.

Nancy nodded. "Excellent scheme! Joey knows girls inside out and she might be able to give us some tips about how to deal with a demon like Jocelyn. She's had experience enough, goodness knows! Look at the time they had with young Margot when she was a Middle!"

Peggy chuckled. "She used to blame all her evil doings on my devil! I've heard her. 'You see, my devil whispered to me.'"

The mistresses giggled at this recollection.

"How like her!" Nancy said.

"Well," Kathy said, hugging her knees, "it's my idea that all this restlessness is growing pains which come on at that stage; and that, my loves, is something we all have to grow out of. Margot is a good sample that way. She's one of our best now."

"She's certainly improved out of all recognition since I first met her in this establishment," Nancy agreed. "So let's hope the same goes for Jocelyn."

There they left it until the Saturday morning when they encountered Mrs Maynard with her three youngest outside the big gate leading on to the highroad.

Joey Maynard, sister of Lady Russell who had started the school on the shores of the Tiernsee—the most beautiful of Tirol's many beautiful lakes—more than twenty-five years before, and whose husband, Dr Jack Maynard, was head of the great Görnetz

Sanatorium, laid proud claim to being the first of the school's pupils. She was also the mother, not only of the Maynard triplets, but of three singleton boys, to quote herself; the twins, Felix and Felicity, her one singleton daughter, and the second batch of twins, Geoffrey and Philippa. In spite of all this she contrived to remain very much of a girl both in character and looks and she always insisted that even if she lived to be a great-grandmother, she would be a Chalet Girl to the end.

As the four converged on her outside the School's two chapels, she gave them a broad grin and waved her hand airily at them.

"Hello people! How goes it?"

"I'm not very sure," Kathy said cautiously. "Hello! You don't mean to say that this bonny young thing is Phil? My word, Joey, she *is* making strides."

Joey laughed. "Isn't she?" She gave a quick look at the family baby. For more than a year little Phil had been the cause of deep anxiety owing to an attack of polio, and even now, when she had been making steady progress for some months, her mother was almost afraid to agree that fears for her were, humanly speaking, at an end.

Kathy saw her look and hastened to change the subject. "Joey, are you engaged to-morrow afternoon?"

"No more than usual. Why?"

"Well, you wouldn't like to entertain us four to tea, would you?"

"Come by all means, provided you'll help with the chores."

"We expect to do that," Nancy laughed. "The fact is, we want some advice."

"Right you are. Plenty of advice on tap, free gratis, too. What's wrong?"

"Wait until to-morrow and you shall hear ALL!" Peggy said dramatically. "I'll tell you this much. It's to do with the Regatta. I'm beginning to feel sorry we decided to revive it."

Joey's black brows shot up. "This is rather strong."

Kathy laughed. "I imagine the present schemozzle is the result of what happened before half-term. I doubt if they'd have thought of it if it hadn't been for that."

"You mean that business with the motor-boat? Ye-es; I suppose we should have expected something to come out of it—at this time of the year, at any rate. Has it inspired the little dears to demand a motor-boat race? Well, they can't have it—or not at this late date. Tell them so."

"Oh, they've been told that—in no uncertain tones, either. But—well, wait till to-morrow and we'll tell you all the details."

Here they were interrupted by Len and Con who came racing up to salute their mother and the family babies, and the mistresses departed on their lawful occasions.

Sunday broke fine and warm and when the four had finished their afternoon duty, they quitted the school premises and strolled along the path above the rock garden, through the rustic gate which had been swung in the hedge which divided the school grounds from those of Freudesheim and up the bank which surrounded the Maynard rose-garden where they found Joey settled under the pines at the far end, with her baby twins curled up on the swing hammock, sheltered from flies by a big mosquito net, and Cecil and the youngest Maynard ward, Claire, sharing a li-lo. All four were asleep, and as she turned to welcome her guests, Joey tapped her lips.

"Sleeping angels!" Nancy said with a grin. "Right! We won't disturb them. But can we move away a little so that we can talk? What about over there near the fountain?"

Joey nodded. "That'll be O.K. Have a Jap sunshade and we'll be comfortable. Fetch a chair, each of you."

They picked up deckchairs from the heap at the farther end of the fountain and set them up, then sat down each with a big Japanese sunshade.

"Now," Joey said when they were settled, "open your budget. I'm all ears—one at a time, please," she added hastily.

Nancy nodded. "I'll begin. Kathy and the rest can shove in any details I miss out!" And she grinned. "It's really the prefects who have felt it as yet, though I'm bound to say that some of those beauties look like playing us up."

"In what way?"

"In making nuisances of themselves."

"What—Erica and Althea? Oh, not Erica, surely!" Joey exclaimed.

"Well—yes and no."

"What on earth do you mean? Either she is or she isn't, and I must say that I never expected that of her. Oh, I don't mean she's an unfledged angel, but I did think she had at least a modicum of common sense."

"I think it's this way," Kathy said, wrinkling up her brows. "She *has* got common sense, but the other two are going head on and as she makes up a trio with them, she feels she must join in."

"But what is it? Begin at the beginning and tell me what it's all about."

"As nearly as I can gather," Nancy said, "those three want motor-boat races. I think they barged in on the prefects' meeting and more or less demanded them, and as the prees were hard at work with very little time to fit everything in, they were refused flatly. Jocelyn cheeked the prees and the other two more or less upheld her."

"Nancy, I simply do not believe Erica backed her up in any impudence—or Althea either, if you come to that. I *can* believe it of Jocelyn. That young demon is like Habakkuk, capable du tout—"

"Yes; and she is leading the other two by the nose."

"Oh, *drat* them!" Joey exclaimed fervently. "What, exactly, are they doing?"

"Sulking, for one thing," Sharlie said.

"In what way?"

"They do what they're told, but most reluctantly," Kathy said. "And they grumble most of the time—under their breath, of course. More than that, they've been trying to get up a party to back them up."

"Oh, confound Jocelyn Marvell!" Joey exploded. "Do you know if she's had any luck? Who did she tackle, by the way?"

"Mainly her own crowd, I believe; but I do know that she also had a go at some of Lower IVb—Val Pertwee, for instance, and that little ass, Marie Angeot. I overheard them talking about it the other day. Also Samaris Davies, who flattened them at once."

"H'm! So far as Samaris is concerned that's what I'd expect. Val is always ready for monkey tricks, about Marie I know nothing. Isn't she that girl who always looks as if she'd just come back from the wash, starched and ironed?"

The mistresses laughed. "She is," Kathy said, "but looks are deceptive."

Then Sharlie threw a minor bombshell into their midst. "Believe it or not, they had a go at Jack Lambert—or so I'm given to understand."

"*What?*" her colleagues exclaimed together.

"Who told you that?" Nancy demanded.

"Well, I got it in a roundabout way from Kit Lucy. She was chattering during our after-church ramble and she was saying that if only Jack would join with Jocelyn and the others the prees might listen to them and it would be such a *smashing* thing to do. Yes; I know you dislike that description, but that was her actual statement."

Joey chuckled. "I'd love to know what Jack had to say to them. She's done some mad things in her own time, but I don't see her backing up anything like this."

"No, you're right there. The trouble is that the Middles are getting all revved up and it's unsettling that part of the School, and just when we want things to go smoothly."

"On the whole," Nancy said judicially, "I wish we'd left the Regatta alone this year."

"Nonsense! It's a pity if the prees, never to mention our noble selves, can't deal with a bunch of malcontents," Kathy retorted.

"Agreed, especially if Joey will bring her weighty mind to bear on the problem."

Joey laughed. "But what sort of advice do you want from me?"

"Well," said Nancy consideringly, "we don't want any hooha that could be avoided. We *could* come down on them, I suppose, but I'd rather calm them down without giving them reason to feel that they're being squashed and have a right to resent the way things are being handled."

"I see. Yes; you're right, of course." Joey thought hard. "I don't know if this will help, but what about getting them together and suggesting that while it can't be done this year, they could be preparing for a shot at it for next. For instance, they might be saving up to make a fund to help pay expenses. That," she added with a wicked grin, "would probably cool their ardour considerably, especially if you pointed out that once they'd begun they must keep on. They might be quite ready to do it for this term, but as there will be no boating next term they aren't likely to be so keen."

Her friends chuckled. "They certainly aren't," Kathy said.

"Well, that would help," Nancy said.

"Try it out," Joey advised. "Remind them that they must have a fund big enough to pay for boat-hire; renting of boat-houses; instruction in handling the boats. Nancy, I'd find out about that if I were you and work out what their subscriptions must be. That would certainly make them stop and think. I don't suppose they've even considered that. By the way, you might suggest it's unlikely they'll get much help from the Games Fund—or would they, Peggy?"

"I don't see how they possibly could. We have enough to do to make it stretch over all we have to do as it is."

"Then there you are. By the way, have you the least idea how many of them want the thing?"

"Not an inkling."

"Then tell them that the first thing to do is to find that out."

"That's all O.K. The trouble is that Jocelyn and Co don't want to wait till next year but get down to it this."

"Then want will have to be their master, I'm afraid. With the best will in the world it couldn't be done. And now," Joey got to her feet, "having advised you to the best of my ability, what about a spot of tea? Who's coming to give me a hand with the trolleys and so on?"

"I will!" All four mistresses jumped up.

"Good! Here come Anna and the Coadjutor to take charge of the family. I thought we might find it easier if they were on duty for once," Joey explained as she turned to welcome her two helpers.

For the next hour or so they forgot about school problems; but when they had finished their meal and were piling up the crockery on the trolleys prior to wheeling them back to the house, Kathy suddenly paused. "I've got another idea."

"Oh; what is it?" Sharlie asked.

"We'll make them keep all the accounts."

"Good heavens; do you think they can?"

"They can with me to oversee them. What's more, they shall learn to do it properly. I'll give them lessons in simple book-keeping. I don't say," she added with a grin, "that they'll like it, but if we make it one of the conditions of running the affair and if they want to do it as badly as that, they'll have to accept our terms."

"Well, it all depends on the Head agreeing to it," Peggy pointed out.

"She'll agree all right," Joey said. "I'll see to that. Let's hope it *larns* them a few things, such as that they can't hope to have such a thing without a lavish supply of extra work. Those blossoms are expecting to have our help and they aren't going to get it. What's more, as we are going to agree to carrying out their wishes—upon terms—they can't sulk or upset the others. That's a jolly good notion, Kathy, and now let's get the crockery back to the house and then we can concentrate on a nice gossip and hope we've solved this problem, at least."

Chapter V

CRUSHING FINALE

"BUT who put all this into your heads?" Miss Annersley looked suspiciously at her mistresses.

"Who do you think? Joey, of course! You surely don't need to be told that!" Nancy Wilmot gave a chuckle.

Miss Annersley laughed. "Yes; it takes her to think up a trick of that kind. Well, I have no objection so long as they understand that it's impossible this year. In fact unless they will undertake to agree to your conditions I shall put a large and heavy foot down on the whole idea. Who are the leaders?"

"It originated with Jocelyn and Co, but they seem to have been canvassing among the Middles and quite a number are keen on it," Kathy said.

"None of the Seniors?"

"Not as far as we know. I do know that the prefects squashed it in no uncertain manner when it was broached to them," Peggy said. "I got that much from Priscilla Dawbarn when I made a few inquiries. I gathered that the squashing was severe and that set up their backs—or Jocelyn's back, anyhow. My own impression is that she is the moving spirit in the affair."

"I'll tell you something I overheard this evening," Miss Moore said. "Len Maynard was standing outside the arbour with Jack Lambert and they were talking hard. Apparently Jocelyn and Co had been on to Jack about their idea, trying to get her to join in with them, and Jack had pointed out that you can't expect mistresses to give up all their free time—the idea was that you, Kathy, were to be asked to train them in the evenings—"

"What? But I haven't a moment to spare just now," expostulated Kathy.

"So Jack seems to have pointed out, but Jocelyn wouldn't see it. Jack was telling Len what she had said and asking her if it was all right."

The Head laughed. "I thought Jack was standing more or less on her own feet now."

"Oh, I think she is; but she still goes to Len for advice if she wants it."

"What did Len say?"

"Said she was quite right. You certainly couldn't take on anything more just now apart from the fact that the thing was impossible for lack of time alone."

A tap at the door interrupted them.

"Entrez!" the Head called; and Len herself came in.

"Oh, I beg your pardon," she said as she glanced at the gathering in the study.

"It's all right," Miss Annersley replied. "I wanted to see you, Len." She nodded to the staff as they rose. "I agree with your ideas and you may carry them out, certainly. I'll see you all in the rock garden after Prayers, shall I?" she added as a bell sounded.

"And there goes the bell for preparation," Nancy said. "Thank you, Miss Annersley." She led the way out of the study and Head Mistress and Head Girl were left alone.

"Come and sit down," Miss Annersley smiled at Len. "Have you come to discuss the question of running motor-boats for the school?"

Len dropped into a chair and gazed at her with wide-open eyes. "Auntie Hilda, who told you?"

"We were just winding up a meeting on the subject."

"O-oh! Then I needn't go into a long explanation." Len gave her a rueful look. "All the same, I rather think we were too crushing at the beginning. You see, we were having a prees' meeting when they landed in on us with this wild idea and we were trying to cram everything we could into the time. We sat heavily on them—too heavily, perhaps. Anyhow, we seem to have upset their little apple-carts." She lapsed from French into English. "And—well, I came to ask you what, if anything, we could do about it. We certainly can't start in on motor-boat races at this late date, but I'd like to set things right if I can."

"I admit it's an awkward situation," the Head said leaning back in her chair. "You're quite right in saying that it can't be done this term. Just how did you squash them? I knew there was something wrong but I've been holding a watching brief in the hope that things would straighten themselves out. As you know, Len, we never like to interfere in your private affairs. Tell me what did happen?"

"Well, it's all off the record," Len began.

"That's understood. You go ahead and tell me the whole story."

Thus encouraged, Len gave a fairly full account of the unhappy prefects' meeting, suppressing all mention of names. When she had finished the Head nodded.

"Yes; whoever was so impudent ought to apologise, but at the moment I think we'll let it go."

Len was in full agreement with this. "It wouldn't do anyone any good if we tried to force that just now. But what are we to do otherwise? You see, Auntie Hilda, those Middles are in a ferment, and it's gone on to some of the Fifth Form now. I know Jack, for one, would adore the idea, though she seems to have seen for herself quite a number of the snags attached. You know, I got quite a shock when she said all that about Miss Ferrars. Jack seems to be growing up in her mind. She wouldn't have worked it out like that this time last year."

"No; but after all she's sixteen in August. It's time she was growing up."

"I suppose so. Well, can you advise us how to deal with that crowd? You see," went on Len, "where Jack and Co were concerned, they did come to us to discuss it, but I don't see people like Jocelyn doing it."

"I think Althea and Erica might, especially if you encouraged them a little."

"Unfortunately we've got off on the wrong foot with them over this motor-boat business. And we can't go back on what we've said. It is simply out of the question from every point of view." Len wrinkled her brows. "It isn't even as if any of *us* could do it. Apart from the fact that we're full up this term, I don't believe any of us—not even Jack who's so mad on cars— could help out."

"Nothing can be done this term. There I fully agree with you. But we've been talking it over with your mother and she's made some suggestions."

Len sat up with a bang. "If you've got Mamma on it I can see a hope. What has she suggested?"

Miss Annersley chuckled. Then she explained what the latest idea was and Len broke into peals of laughter.

"Oh, Auntie Hilda! That ought to calm them down a little. And it's such plain sense. When are you going to tell them?"

"After Abendessen."

"Good! If you make it as official as all that they'll have to stop and think."

"Exactly. Well, I have a lecture with Va in ten minutes' time so I'm turning you out. Meantime, if you can spare a short time to consider it with the rest you had better be off. And do what you can, all of you, to get them to accept that it is only on conditions of this kind that we can agree to it for next summer."

Len jumped up. "Everything we can. Life has been trying with them since we came back and this is the end of our schooldays and we all wanted to make them good. Oh, dear! Half of me is looking forward to Oxford, but half of me doesn't like the thought that this part of my life is over."

"You'll find that happening all through your life, my child. We can never stand still. We must go on. It's our affair whether we make a better show of it, or go back and let everyone down, ourselves included."

The conversation ceased there, but Len went to the prefects' room, where she settled down to make notes for an essay, with intervals of telling the others what was proposed for dealing with the latest trouble in the school.

"That should bring them to their senses," Margot said.

"And as it comes from the Head it should put a stop to all the bother we've been having," Ted added.

Con finished copying out a quotation. Then she laid down her pen. "And thank goodness, the Regatta comes at the end of this month and then we can get down to the Sale. And now I've piles of work still to do, so do you think we *could* give the Regatta a miss and have a little silence until the end of prep?"

The others laughed at her tone, but as all of them had work to do, they buckled down to preparation for the time being.

By mutual consent no one mentioned motor-boats during Abendessen. People at the heads of tables steered the conversation to other topics. Len, at the head of the table round which Upper IVb was seated, steered them off on the subject of the Sale by wondering if their annual doll's house would be forthcoming this year. It was made, decorated, and furnished by an Old Girl, Tom Gay, and was regarded as one of the chief money draws at the Sale. Tom was a trained carpenter, and she made a habit of pulling in all her friends and relatives to help. No one ever knew just what form it would take. One year she had provided an Elizabethan house. Another time she had produced a village, complete with manor house, church, village inn, and horse-pond (made of a small mirror). As Tom's gift was always elaborate, it was made the subject of a competition set by Tom, and Len's tactful introduction of this set most of them discussing it. Other tables, overhearing, took it up, and for the time being most people forgot motor-boat races in the interest of trying to guess what Tom could have provided this year.

At the end of the meal the Head stood up and rang the little electric bell near to her hand. At once there was silence and the girls turned their eyes to where she stood, wondering what was to come.

"I have something to say to you, girls," she said, smiling at them. "I hear that some of you people want to have a motor-boat race in the Regatta. I think it might be quite a good idea. Unfortunately, you thought of it too late. Now wait. How many of you know anything about handling a motor-boat? Hands up."

One hand went up—Jocelyn's. "I had a little practice during the half-term."

"Yes? How much?"

"My uncle took my aunt and me out three times," Jocelyn said. "He said I should be good very quickly. All I needed was practice. Truly, Miss Annersley, I found it easy."

"How far did you go each time?"

Jocelyn fidgetted. "Well—not a long way, of course."

"Was he beside you all the time?"

"Yes; but he only told me what to do and the third time he didn't even do that, not once I'd started her."

The Head laughed. "It sounds very well, Jocelyn, but I'm afraid it's not enough. I expect he took you to a very quiet spot where you were unlikely to meet other boats. And that is all?"

"Ye-es," Jocelyn faltered, very red.

"My dear girl, it's not nearly enough. Surely you can see that for yourself. And if you have had that much practice, what about the others who have not even had that? I'm very sorry, Jocelyn, but I'm afraid that from that point of view alone, I can't give consent. But there are other reasons. How do you propose to pay for the hire of boats—the rent of boat-houses, petrol and oil, service? Motor-boat racing is an expensive hobby. Then we should have to get someone to train you and that would be another expense. Had you thought of that?"

"Couldn't Miss Ferrars take that over? She knows about motor-boats."

"Of course not. Miss Ferrars is here to teach Junior and Middle School maths and geography mainly. If she likes to give a hand with games we are all very grateful to her, but it is not her real job and such time as she does give to it she takes out of her free time."

Kathy Ferrars, who had been looking horrified at the suggestion, relaxed.

"Thank goodness the Head has sense!" she murmured to Sharlie Andrews.

Miss Annersley caught the murmur, smiled at the young mistress and then proceeded to launch another bombshell at the motor-boat enthusiasts. "Of course, if we did fall in with your suggestion, you must understand that such a thing would be an extra as much as music, or ballet dancing, or extra languages and must be charged for accordingly. I doubt if many of your parents would care for that."

This again was something that none of them had thought of. Even Jocelyn began to feel that there was an awful number of snags connected with her wonderful idea.

The Head watched her vivid little face keenly. "You see," she said gently, "there are so many things to consider when you start a thing like this. I'm sorry, girls, but I'm afraid it simply can't be done. Certainly not at once. You'll have to give it up—for the present, anyhow. In fact, I'm going to suggest that you give up all thought of it just now and concentrate on other interests. You've plenty to occupy your minds for the rest of the term. Our present Regatta arrangements, our Sports and our Sale of Work. But I'm going to propose that during the holidays those of you who can should try to get a little practice on motor-boating. You never know what the future may bring, and if you can come back next term knowing more about what you want to tackle, it will be all to the good. Now that is all. Stand!"

The girls stood at once, and after grace she dismissed them to clear the tables and then to collect their deckchairs and go out to the grounds to settle down for their regular half-hour's rest. They streamed off, and presently the shady nooks were filled with girls armed with books, since talking was forbidden at this time.

Once the rest period was over there was no time for chatter. The afternoon was filled up with games and sports practice and, for most of the upper forms, work in languages, needlework, science and art. Most of the girls had more than enough to think of, but Jocelyn, engaged with the rest of her form in a lesson on design with Miss Yolland the Art mistress, gave little of her mind to it and narrowly escaped being turned out of the art-room. Althea and Erica managed better. For one thing, although the idea had attracted them, they were by no means as crazy about it as Jocelyn. For another, neither was of the same wholesale character as their partner in crime.

"I can't see why you want to go on after what the Head said," Erica remarked. "It won't do any good, anyhow. Give it a rest, Jos, do!"

Jocelyn eyed her scornfully. "Is that all you can say? Give in like good little girls and let the prees think they've got the better of us! Well, that may be you, but it isn't me."

Althea considered. "No; but if it won't do any good why waste time that way? So far as I am concerned, I'm going to dig in at the things we *can* do this year."

"Ditto me," Erica agreed. "You can't say the Head turned it down absolutely. I think," she added, "that she's been very fair about it. And, you know, she's quite right in one way. I don't suppose our people will be anxious to pay for an extra like that. Anyhow, I know Auntie Joey won't, so that settles it for me, anyhow."

"Garrh!" snarled Jocelyn. "The fact is you're funking the fuss you think will follow if we stick it out."

"No, we're not," retorted Althea. "We've got a little more common sense than you, that's all."

How this argument might have ended is anyone's guess, but at that point Margot joined them to ask why they were not on the tennis courts where they ought to have been, and even Jocelyn hesitated to rouse the Games prefect's rasping tongue. The trio went to the courts, followed by Margot, who proceeded to summon Samaris Davies from the practice boards to make up a doubles, and then gave them a sound coaching which gave them little or no time to think of anything but tennis.

Jack Lambert watched them for a few minutes and decided that since the Head had put paid to the idea she need not worry about Jocelyn and Co for the moment, so turned her attention to her own concerns. Only Len Maynard spared time to wonder if the three would be held by the Head's decision for longer than the moment.

Later on, when the Middles had departed to bed, and the Seniors strolled about the grounds chatting among themselves, Ted, Len and Carmela perched themselves on the wall running across the rock garden and discussed the matter seriously.

"You know," Len said, "practically none of us will be here next term. We three will be at the university. Jeanne and Primrose and Marie and at least fifteen of VIb will be Millies. Ruey Richardson is going to Bedford to begin her P.T. training and Melanie Lucas is hoping to join her people in New York."

"What's she going to do?" Carmela asked.

"It's wrop in Mystry," Ted said with a giggle.

"What on earth do you mean?"

"Just that. There's one thing she *won't* do—that is sing like her mother."

The other two laughed. "I imagine not," Len said. "Oh, I don't say she has *no* voice, but she's got no more than most of us and Mrs Lucas is a prima donna."

"Ever heard her?" Carmela queried.

"Yes—about two years ago. Her voice is lovely, but Melanie's is just ordinary."

"Hard luck on her people. But why bring that up now?" Ted asked.

"I was thinking of next term."

"What *about* next term?"

"Well, hasn't it struck you two yet that practically all the prefects will be new?"

"That's what usually happens in Christmas term, my love. It's nothing new," Ted reminded her. "But there will be quite a number of VIb left to take our places. Most of Va will be promoted to VIb not to speak of a fairish number of the present VIb to take our places in VIa."

"I know; but I'd like to start them off decently. We had Maeve Bettany and Betty Landon and Alicia Leonard and Pen Grant and a lot of other people. And our crowd had a good deal of training from them; not to speak of the people who came immediately before them."

"You stop worrying about them," Ted said severely. "They'll have to find their own feet, just as we did. Honestly, Len, you're incorrigible!"

Len coloured and then laughed. Carmela looked up at them and raised her black brows. "But why?" she asked. "Why is Len incorrigible?"

"Worrying about other people," Ted explained. "She *will* do it. Hello! There's the bell. Time we were retiring to bed. Let's hope we have a peaceful night."

"Don't we usually?"

"We do." Carmela slipped a hand in the arm of each and they sauntered back to the house.

"We do—unless Con starts sleep walking. I'll grant you," said Ted solemnly, "that we can usually reckon on a shock of some kind when that happens. But she seems to have given it up for the time being, at all events."

They were mounting the stairs by this time to the upper corridors where the Seniors were moving quietly to their dormitories. Matron was walking quickly along to her own room and said a smiling goodnight to them. The prefects parted company and Len, who as Head Girl had a small room to herself, went into her own abode after murmuring goodnight to her triplet sisters who appeared at that moment. Half-an-hour later except for one or two of the mistresses' rooms and the Head's private drawingroom, everything was in darkness and peace settled down on the School.

Chapter VI

AN UNEXPECTED ADVENTURE

On the whole things went quietly for the remainder of the week. What with lessons, games, swimming and rowing practice, and odd moments for finishing off their offerings for the Sale, no one had much time for anything else. The Head having stamped heavily on the proposed motor-boat race, even Jocelyn gave it up for the time being and concentrated instead on rowing and swimming. Consequently she became considerably easier to live with.

The weather had become cooler though it was still hot enough for most folk, as Con remarked. "Let's hope it isn't the forerunner of thunderstorms," she added as she swept her black hair back from her face. "You know what can happen then!" However, any thunderstorms in the offing remained there for the time being.

On Sunday the girls went to early services in their own two little chapels, after which Miss Annersley ordained rambles for everyone as long as they kept in the shade wherever possible.

"Karen and Co were at work earlier and you may take picnic meals with you. Keep to the shelf and our own woods," she said when announcing the decision. "Take your books with you and have a quiet, restful day of it. Yes, Renata?"

"May we also take our needlework with us?" Renata asked demurely.

"Certainly; also sketchblocks and paintboxes. The only thing is I don't wish you to rush about. This hot weather is trying and we've had it for more than a week on end, now." She glanced round the room, saw that everyone was ready, and gave the word for Grace before dismissing them to table-clearing and bed-making.

By half-past-nine all the odd chores were finished and the girls were congregating in their various forms on the path round the school, each form with two or three prefects and a couple of mistresses in charge. Len was in charge of Upper IVa with Eve Hurrell as her pair and Mdlle de Lachennais and Miss Ferrars. It was a biggish form as forms at the Chalet School went and also contained some of the worst firebrands in the place. Len was just setting the lines in order for marching off when Miss Wilmot arrived, followed by the members of Upper IVa and wearing an apologetic air.

"Oh, do you people mind having this crowd tacked on to you for once?" the head of the mathematics branch asked Len. "We're sending Primrose Trevoase and Audrey Everett along, too, but the Head wants to see us and this seems the only available time. Can you manage, do you think, Len?"

"Of course," Len said readily, "and Miss Ferrars and Mdlle de Lachennais are coming, too."

"I'm sorry," Miss Wilmot said, "but I'm afraid they aren't. The Head wants them as well. But you can have any Seniors who are free to help out."

This improved matters. Len looked round hurriedly. "May I have Jack Lambert and Wanda von Eschenau and—and Janice Chester?"

"By all means. Sure that'll be enough?"

"Oh, ample!"

"Very well. I'll send them along." She turned to her charges. "Girls! Remember this is Sunday and a day of quiet. I don't want to hear any bad reports. Don't give Len and the others reason for handing any in to me." Then she turned and hurried back along the path while the prefects waved to the newcomers to take their places in the lines. By the time the three Seniors had arrived quite a number of the crocodiles had moved off. Len made no delay but gave the word, and the two Upper IV forms, laden with rucksacs, oddments such as books, needlework and art materials, were going briskly forward towards the highroad.

"Where are we going, Len?" asked Erica as they rounded the bend.

"To the Auberge and beyond," Len said. "It ought to be cool by the stream if anywhere and there are all those pines along the bank to give us shade. We don't often go there, so I thought it would be a change."

A quick chorus of delight greeted her statement.

"Oh, mais c'est une bonne idée!" exclaimed Marie Angeot.

"Oh, goody-goody!" cried Erica. "Not that there'll be much water in the fall," she added. "I should think the stream is more or less bone-dry after all the heat we've been having. Still it is somewhere fairly fresh."

The others joined in and Len beamed. It had been a sudden inspiration on her part while she was making her bed and she had torn down to the Head to ask if anyone else wanted the place and had been overjoyed to hear that no one had thought of it or asked for it.

"Only be careful about letting them climb about the bed," Miss Annersley warned her. "That is a very rocky river bed and you don't want any accidents that can be avoided. Matron will give you the usual first-aid box and the people at the Auberge will be ready to give you a helping hand in case of need."

There it was left and the party set out full of the anticipation of joys to come.

So long as they were on the shelf they must march in crocodile, and that meant half way along the Platz to where the mountain railway line cut it. Here they turned down for a short distance before swinging round a great clump of bushes into a rock-walled passage. The left-hand wall came to a sudden end and the girls gazed delightedly across the valley in which Interlaken stands, to the great range of the Berner Alps. The path ran on round the mountain. The Seniors led the way, warning the younger girls to keep close to the slope, for the path was not wide, though quite a good part was protected at the edge by a low natural wall of rock. At length they came to a cove which held a long low building with frescoed walls, tucked comfortably under the slope of the mountain. In front of it was a courtyard fenced round on three sides with stout wooden rails set closely together. There was a gate on either side, but across the front the fencing gave no access to the courtyard.

The girls knew the secret of the Auberge and once they were safely enclosed they raced to the front fence and proceeded to set up a variety of noises, from simple "Coo-ee!" which satisfied a fair number to Primrose's ambitious effort, "Lo, hear, the gentle lark". Each noise was returned again and again, every repeat growing fainter and fainter, but always miraculously sweet. It was not new to most of them, but it never lost its fascination.

"But you ought to hear it when we have someone really musical with us," Robina McQueen told Althea, to whom it *was* new. "That really is something."

"I think it's marvellous as it is," Althea said fervently.

"Well, come on now," Eve said. "I don't know about you people, but I'm hungry and I want Mittagessen."

"What's the matter with having it here?" Althea demanded.

"We could, of course, but we don't as a rule, in case the Auberge gets a sudden rush of tourists. I think we'll go outside as usual. Come on! Line up and let's get cracking," Primrose said. "By the way, keep out of the river bed."

"Why?" demanded Clarissa Dendy, a shining light of Lower IVb.

"Well, you just look at it and you'll *see* why, if you've any eyes in your head," Len told her. "Look at those rocks and boulders. They're enough to sprain your ankle or break your collar-bone if you tripped over that lot. And how, I ask you, do you imagine we should get you back to school? No, thank you! We'll be safe and *not* sorry on this occasion, thank you!"

Len spoke with a firmness there was no gainsaying. All the same, as the girls patrolled along the bank of the little river, Audrey Everett confided sotto voce to her great friend Primrose, "I'm extremely thankful that Jocelyn Marvell is not among this crowd. Can you hear her taking a dictum of that kind without an argument? I can't!"

"Oh, I daresay she would in the long run," Primrose said casually. "Aren't you rather giving a dog a bad name and hanging him? I know she's made a little pest of herself, but she's been better this last day or two."

"Anyhow, it's partly her age," said Len who had overheard this. "Earliest 'teens are a very tiresome age." She gave a rueful grin. "I know I got plenty of tickings off when I was at that stage and most of them well deserved, too. Come to that, I'll bet you weren't exactly an angel yourself. And as for your young Celia we all know what she's been like. You pipe down a bit about Jocelyn, Audrey."

Audrey grinned back. "Too true, all of it. Well, I'm getting tired of this scrambling and I have a hollow vacancy inside me that is yelling for whatever it is Karen has put up for us. How will this do for a pleasing spot for a picnic?"

"Most pleasing." Len raised her voice. "We'll feed here, I think. Find seats and settle down, everyone."

It was a kind of dingle with plenty of grassy spaces and some large boulders to be used as chairbacks. The girls quickly settled down and proceeded to unpack their knapsacks. Karen and the kitchen staff had provided as lavishly as usual. There were fresh rolls thickly buttered and sandwiched with slices of savoury meat and lettuce; hard-boiled eggs to eat with them; cartons of strawberries, sugared and creamed; to top up, a large slice each of Karen's special cake. To drink there was a fruit drink made from one of the school's own recipes. The girls enjoyed it all and when it was finished they cleared up, tucking everything neatly away, and then Len announced a half-hour's rest and most of them settled down to quiet chatter, though one or two produced books and Clare Kynaston and Emmy Friedrich unashamedly went to sleep.

The end of the half-hour saw the majority of them ready for activity, however, though Len looked up at the sky with her brows knitted.

"What's wrong?" Primrose asked her as they piled up the repacked rucksacs under a clump of tall pines.

"I don't exactly like the look of the sky," Len said.

"What? There's nothing wrong with it, is there?" Primrose looked up in her turn.

"I'm not sure. We're rather shut in here. It looks all right overhead but look in that corner. It's got rather a brassy look."

Primrose gazed at the corner, then she suddenly smiled and waved. "Look, Len! There's Dr Entwistle!"

Len waved to the tall young fellow who had come round a bend in the river. He waved back and then quickened his pace. "I say, do you girls know what the sky's like over there? Better get this crowd back to the Auberge. We're in for a snorter or I'm much mistaken. Who's on duty with you?"

"Our noble selves," Len said, springing to her feet. "The Head wanted the staff so we're in charge. Are you sure, Reg?"

"As sure as makes no matter," he replied, joining her. "Get those kids together and move them off before it comes. It'll be a snorter when it does or my name's not Reg Entwistle." With this he turned to helping to sling rucksacs over small shoulders and the big girls backed him up ably.

"Rain on the way," Len called. "Pick up all your belongings.

You can't come back for lost or left things. If we have what I expect, all this part will be flooded in half no time. Whose is that book? Grab it."

Freda Kendal snatched it and then in response to an imperative wave of Reg's arm scrambled up the bank to the path leading to the Auberge. The Seniors had already got all the other girls there, and Eve and Primrose were marshalling them into line, while Audrey was counting as they began to march past. Meanwhile the doctor was standing listening. Suddenly he swung round.

"Get on!" he shouted. "Get on to the Auberge! Hurry!"

There was an urgency in his voice which set them running as fast as they could. *Why* they should run they had no idea. They only knew that they must. At the same moment they heard a distant rumble like thunder which yet was not thunder. Reg Entwistle came tearing up. Len was at the end of the crocodile and he flung an arm round her as he came up.

"*Run!*" he said tensely.

Len said nothing, but seeing that the last of the younger girls had reached the upper path she left the care of them to her three fellow prefects and devoted herself to scrambling as fast as she could up to the level of the Auberge, the doctor urging her on as hard as he could. The faces of both were white, for both had guessed at the explanation for the ever-increasing thunder which was descending the slopes of the mountain. They reached the path and as Reg lifted Len up to it, the noise seemed to be reaching its climax. Len was breathless and he was almost as bad, but he still rushed the girl on, willy-nilly.

"I—*can't!*" Len gasped out as her knees gave way and she nearly went headlong.

"You must!" he snapped, hauling her to both feet again. "Get on!"

At his tone Len found enough strength to go on, but she never knew where it came from. She was shaking, partly with tiredness, partly with fear. Then as she dragged herself round a giant pine and he pushed her on, she glanced round and saw a sight which she never forgot and which haunted her nightmares for years to come. Bearing down on the stream came a wall of yellowish water, crusted with yeasty foam, swirling higher and higher up the trunks of the trees so that the lower branches were submerged and the bank up which they had clambered so madly was hidden beneath the torrent. It mounted nearer and nearer their path and behind that first awful wave others were coming, almost as awful.

Then, even as she looked, she saw one great pine go crashing down under the force of the water. Two more followed, and already the foam was swirling round her own and Reg's knees. If it had not been for his arm clasped firmly round her waist the girl felt that she must have gone down, but miraculously he steadied her and somehow got her up to a higher ledge. At the same moment the worst of the flood passed, though what followed was still terrifying enough.

Reg glanced down at her white face. "Don't you dare to faint here!" he flung at her. "You've got to keep up because of the kids. You can't leave it all to Primrose and the others. Keep going!"

Len set her teeth and pulled herself together. "O.K. I've got my breath now. We're past the worst of the scramble, anyhow. The Auberge is safe, too, that's clear, so the kids must be safe. I'm sure they all got there in time."

"Right! Let's join them and make certain, though."

She was willing enough, but she was in very poor shape by this time and it took some minutes before they reached the gate and were instantly seized on by Primrose and Jack Lambert.

"Thank God you're safe!" was all Primrose said; but that very boyish young person, Jack Lambert, flung her arms round Len and burst into a storm of tears such as no one had ever seen Jack indulge in.

"Oh, Len—Len! I th-thought you w-were d-drowned!" she wept.

Len gave her a hug. "Well, I'm not! Oh, I do fe-el so—" She got no further, for at that point nature gave out and she collapsed. Reg's arms were ready and he staggered into the Auberge with her amid the wails of the girls, while Primrose dashed to the telephone and rang up the Sanatorium, demanding an ambulance, nurses and other doctors instanter, and the mistress of the Auberge got Len carried to a bedroom by her husband, and then proceeded to strip her of her soaked clothing and tuck her up in bed.

Dr Maynard was at the Sanatorium when Primrose's call came through and he put matters in hand at once. When Len finally came round completely which was not for some time, her father was beside her and Dr Entwistle had been marched off to the Sanatorium to be treated for a wrenched back muscle, the result of his exertions, and the girls were packed off to the school to be dealt with by the authorities there for strained nerves.

Joey, as it happened, was spending the weekend down at Vevey, so knew nothing about it until she returned home on the Tuesday, by which time the girls were beginning to recover from the shock; even Len, who had been kept in bed, looked more like herself. But Jack did not soon recover from having made, as she said, "a watering can ninny" of herself; and Reg Entwistle had a week or two of aching back to endure. Len was no light weight, for all her slenderness, and he had strained himself severely in lifting her to safety.

Chapter VII

ACCIDENT

ON the whole, once they had recovered from the shock, Upper IV a and b were inclined to preen themselves on their adventure. No one else in the school had met with anything like it. One or two nervy people were affected by nightmares for the next few weeks, but on the whole they recovered quickly. For one thing the school saw to it that there was little or no time for brooding. For another the open envy of quite a number of people of other forms turned their minds in another direction from fear. Finally, Miss Ferrars explained to them during her geography lessons what had been the cause of it.

"It was caused by the breaking down of the dam at one side of that little lake on the Rösleinalp, and that was caused by a cloudburst a little further up the slope," she said. "It's the sort of thing that can happen once in a lifetime. In any case the authorities are attending to it and it's unlikely to happen again."

"Once is enough for me," shuddered Primrose when she heard this. "I don't want another ghastly experience of that kind!"

"Well, you didn't get the worst of it," Ted pointed out. "Snap out of it, Primrose."

Primrose said no more and the talk died down. But among the elder girls there arose a new topic. It began with Zita Roselli of VIb who, cocking a shrewd eye to the visits paid by Dr Entwistle to Freudesheim, was moved to suggest that there was something between him and Len Maynard.

"Nonsense!" said Ruey Richardson to whom Zita was talking. "Len is far too busy for anything like that. What's more, if the

Head caught you talking in that way she'd have something to say about it."

"But why?" Zita protested. "After all, Len is nearly eighteen and that is not too young."

"Well, we don't talk of things like that," Ruey said.

All the same, the idea caught on and spread among the Seniors, especially the younger members of VIb and Va, where the majority of the girls were Continentals and accustomed to early betrothals. The talk was very much *sub rosa* at the moment, for the policy of the school was to keep the girls clear of such gossip until they left school proper. The Heads considered that with all the work they were expected to do the less their minds were deflected the better. As for the Maynard family, Joey had always tended to keep her girls young, and neither she nor Jack Maynard wanted any of their three to be thinking about marriage at the present. As far as Len herself was concerned she was, to all seeming, uninterested, and when Dolores Zaragova of Va hinted at it, Len froze up to her stateliest and administered such a snubbing that Dolores was utterly crushed and dared say no more.

All the same, Len seemed to become more inaccessible to her contemporaries and even her sisters were not sure what to think. Not that they discussed it either. But the term was hurrying by and when it ended Len and the others would be leaving school, for all three were to go to University in October.

And then something happened which drove the whole thing out of their minds for the time being.

It began with Jane Carew of Inter V producing a temperature. Matron, with an eye to the rest of the school, promptly sent her into isolation where she was joined two days later by two more members of Inter V and on the next day by Melanie Lucas of Vb and then, just as the Head was on the point of separating the Senior school from the rest, no fewer than five of the Junior Middles, including Marta Wilhelm and Felicity Maynard followed suit.

"Oh, my *goodness*!" wailed Peggy Burnett when she heard the news, "What happens now? And what *is* it, for pity's sake?"

That was something that no one seemed to be prepared to state. That it was infectious was clear enough, but apart from the temperature which, in nearly every case was not very high but obstinate, there were few symptoms. The girls were none of them seriously ill, but do what they would, the temperature remained as a worrying factor. The doctors fought it but seemed unable to conquer it. Matron dosed the patients with nostrums of her own, but could make no headway. Further, more cases were coming up. The school's private sanatorium was crammed and Nurse had commandeered two dormitories as extensions, for the mysterious disease was now running through the school from top to bottom. The day appointed for the Regatta finals saw eleven new patients in Nurse's charge and the Regatta itself cancelled.

By this time the Sanatorium had called in people from the hospitals in Lucerne and other medical centres, for whatever the germ was which had invaded the Platz baffled them completely. What was worse, the infection had begun to spread outside the School. The trouble began to clear up there by the end of a fortnight, but it had killed the Regatta. For some reason beyond most folk, this reconciled Jocelyn to having to forgo her cherished project of a motor-boat race and returned her to a mood of pleasantness.

"And that," said Len thoughtfully, "means look out for squalls."

However, by the time Jocelyn might have been ripe for mischief they were deep in preparations for the Sale. She herself was thrilled to have been chosen for Puck in the Midsummer episode, which meant that she must be the Messenger for Summer's stalls and was likely to be on the move most of the time, instead—to quote herself—of "having to stick around as saleswoman at some stall or other and do the polite".

"Not to speak of having to work out sums of money for change," Robina put in.

Jocelyn, whose arithmetic was on the legendary side, grimaced at Robina but let it go at that.

The next event, however, put most things out of their minds. It began with one of the maids missing the last train up from the valley. Unfortunately, she had no money with her so was unable to ring up the school to explain. She decided that she had better walk up to the Platz, and set out accordingly. It was not a difficult walk and not dangerous, for the night was fine with a glorious midsummer moon; but it took some time and when Gretchen finally reached the school everyone was in bed and asleep.

Gretchen was dismayed at the prospect of waking someone to let her in. More or less the same thing had happened a fortnight before and Karen had not spared her tongue. What she would say at this repeat, Gretchen dared not think. She decided that her best plan was to see if she could find admittance at some window left unlatched. Then, if the worst came to the worst, she could curl up in some corner until the morning and do her best to pacify her particular tyrant by at least not having disturbed anyone else.

Normally, it was most unlikely that any admittance to the school would be available. On this occasion, however, someone had been careless and Gretchen finally discovered a window left unlatched in one of the storerooms. She contrived to scramble in, dropped to the floor, and then found that she was not much better off. The storeroom was not only bolted on the outside but also locked. Karen was taking no chances.

To make matters worse, having got in there was no getting out again. Neither was there any prospect of comfort, for this was the storeroom for such things as the great flourbins, and the floor seemed to be the only prospect of bed for her.

Gretchen was tired with her lengthy walk. She was also, by this time, both hungry and thirsty and she was only sixteen. When she finally discovered her dilemma, she plumped down on the floor and burst into tears.

The storeroom was beneath the maids' dormitories and most of them, being healthy young females, slept soundly after their day's work and were not easily roused. Once she had given way Gretchen did it thoroughly. She howled loudly and presently the noise she made reached Matron Henschell of St Agnes'. Barbara Henschell was an old pupil of the School and she was out of bed very speedily and into her dressing-gown and bedroom slippers in short order.

She scurried out of her room along the corridor in such haste that she forgot to tie her dressing-gown cord securely. It came loose, she caught her foot in it and went headlong down the stairs. Barbara was a buxom person and went with a crash, catching her right arm in the banisters as well as banging her head forcibly against the stair-rail with a vim which knocked her out for the moment.

What with Gretchen's howls, Barbara's exclamations in the first shock of her fall and when she came round, before long the entire school was completely roused. Luckily Dr Maynard was at home and in a few minutes after he had received a hurried phone call from the school, he arrived to attend to the victim of the affair. His verdict was that Barbara was suffering from a compound fracture of the right arm, complicated by slight concussion, and that she would not be fit for duty for the next two or three weeks.

In the meantime Gretchen had been released by Karen. What she proceeded to say to her had to be heard to be believed. By the time the kitchen tyrant had finished, what was left of the girl would have gone into a thimble and the rest of the kitchen staff was on its toes. To make matters worse, the kitchen cat took advantage of the confusion to slip out. Minette was beloved by most folk and quite a number of people went hunting for her. By the time she was safely in her basket dawn had come, half the night had gone, and Matey, after a brief consultation with Miss Annersley, had ordained that the rising bell should not be rung for two hours and, which found no favour with the girls, bed should come an hour and a half earlier than usual.

Next morning Miss Annersley held a conference with the remaining matrons as to the best way to manage during the few weeks remaining of the term. They were all of the opinion that it was not worth while engaging a temporary matron and that they could arrange Barbara's duties among themselves, especially as two of the prefects offered to help out. Kirsten Johansen was headed for work as a housekeeper when her schooldays and training were over, and Gabrielle Maynolles of VIb meant to go in for Motel keeping and offered her services eagerly. Apart from this, St Agnes House as a whole was on its mettle, and appeared to have every intention of behaving like a set of models as far as in it lay.

Nurse would be responsible for the health side of the matter and that would be everything settled.

"It's a horrid mix-up," Miss Annersley said when it was all tied up. "However, it's the best we can arrange, and now we *must* give our minds to the public exams and the Sale. But *what* a term this is!"

All this was on the Friday. On the Saturday the upper school was set in order for the public exams and the Senior school from VIb down to Vb were fully occupied. In weather like the present the girls were working out of doors unless the forecast was really bad. In order to ensure quiet, the end-of-the-term exams were also held, so everyone was up to the eyes in work.

In the afternoon lessons were set aside. If you were not fully prepared by that time you never would be. Books were locked away and after Mittagessen and their customary rest, everyone was sent to form clumps of a score or so girls in charge of a mistress or a couple of prefects. Each group was sent off to picnic either in the woods or some niche along the shelf with strict injunctions to keep out of mischief, avoid the heated areas and be back in school by 18.00 hours. Joey Maynard invited the entire Junior School to spend the afternoon and evening at Freudesheim, which accounted for seventy girls. She claimed the services of her own triplets and the Heads thankfully agreed.

There was one mercy. By this time the mysterious malady had more or less ended and the two people in the school sanatorium were there for a twisted ankle and a bilious attack, the direct result of a midnight in one of the dormitories, and an orgy of cake and tinned sardines, and that was easily dealt with by the Matron in charge of the dormitory. The invalid was dosed with the school's special bilious nostrum and the lady with the twisted ankle was firmly bandaged and ordered to keep her foot up for the next two or three days until the ankle had healed. As for the orgiasts, they too were dosed, and by the time they had got rid of the taste of those doses they were feeling sorry they had ever thought of the feast. That mixture was not only disgusting, it was *lingering*, and all they were given them to get rid of the worst of it was drinks of water.

So Monday came and with it exams.

Chapter VIII

THE PICNIC THAT NEVER CAME OFF

ON the Sunday evening of that week, the staff commandeered the entire Middle school to help set out the desks and chairs in the grounds, in readiness for next week's exams and tests. The public exams would take place in Hall so that must wait till early Monday morning; but the weather forecasts were all good so it was decided to prepare the outdoor arrangements as far as possible. They would use the long trestle tables with safety inkwells, and there were plenty of spare folding chairs. The prefects took charge, and while Ted Grantley collected the members of the two Upper Fourths and set them to carrying out the tables and putting them up, Eve Hurrell, Marie Huber, Maria Zinkel and Louise Grunbaum took charge of Lower IV and IIIa and saw to the carrying out of the chairs and placing them round the tables.

"We won't set the inkwells out," Len decided, "but we can get them filled ready."

"Where are we keeping them?" Con asked.

"Somewhere safe, I hope," Priscilla Dawbarn remarked. "We don't want half the youngsters douching themselves with ink!"

"Matey would have something to say," giggled Margot. "What about asking Deney if we can keep them in one of the stockrooms?"

"That's a notion. Good for you, Margot! They should be safe enough from the kids there," agreed Len. "Look here, I'll go and see if I can catch her while the rest of you see to the setting-out. Then we'll get the inkwell trays."

"And Jeanne and Carmela can get the ink and begin filling the wells. How many shall we need, do you think?"

"Deney will tell us that. She has the registers. Do we allow one between two or must they have one each?"

"Oh, one each, my love. You never can rely on what the Middles and Juniors might do if two of them made a dive for the same inkwell. And safety or not, you can't be sure there wouldn't be spills in that case."

"It *has* happened before now," Con assented. "O.K. Let's hope we have enough. Luckily we can leave all Seniors out of it."

"Why? Are they to be allowed to use ballpoint pens? Lucky they! *We* never were." This was Eve.

"I haven't heard of it. I was only referring to the fact that VIb and V a and b are all in for one or other of the public exams so will be in the Hall and using the folding desks. And that reminds me, don't forget that those inkwells have to be filled sooner or later as well," Len said from the doorway where she had paused.

"In that case it'll be later if I have any say in the matter," Con remarked firmly. "You get off and find Deney and get all the needed data from her and we'll carry on with the rest of the jobs."

"O.K." Len vanished and the rest of the prefects turned to with a will.

The Middles also turned to. They had already been warned that they had none too much time to do everything and on the morrow they would be busy with heats for various races. Jocelyn got down to work without a grumble. She had learned during her time at school to refrain from making rude remarks about having to fag at this sort of thing.

"You may *think* what you like!" Samaris Davies had told her crushingly. "Thought is free after all. But if your thoughts are no more sensible than the ones you've been expressing, keep them to yourself. Life's too full for us to waste time over what isn't sensible or decent."

Jocelyn had given a loud sniff and marched off, vowing that Samaris Davies was a specious pig and she would have nothing more to do with her—which lasted for about half a day. Samaris was an attractive creature even to a girl who was all too apt to carry a chip on her shoulder at the least thing.

By the time the bell rang for Prayers everything was done and when they were over the girls set to work collecting and sorting the various offerings for the Sale. As it was the collection of a year's work there was a goodly showing. The school prided itself on its needlework, both plain and fancy. You might hate the very sight and touch of a needle but you were well and truly taught to use one.

Len, counting a pile of pillow-cases, commented on this fact. "I will say for this school it turns us out decent needlewomen," she observed.

Margot giggled. "You've little chance of becoming anything else, what with Mdlle, Matey and the housemistresses. Even Mamma can sew and goodness knows there never existed anyone who loathed the job more than she has always done."

"Listen to the pot calling the kettle black," Con cried. They three and Carmela were strolling round the sunken garden by this time, admiring the rock plants that walled it round, Len having finished her counting of pillow-cases for the time being.

Margot laughed. "Oh, I've never pretended to like it and I'll admit that when I was a kid I hated it from the depths of my heart. But I don't mind admitting now that I'm very glad I was made to learn it properly, like it or not."

Con flashed her a queer look. "You said that about drawing and painting. Do you expect everything to come in handy with your future job?"

Margot nodded vigorously. "Everything!"

Carmela looked at her thoughtfully. "You're going in for medicine. How do you expect art and needlework to help out?"

Margot's fair face crimsoned. "Because what I'm aiming at in the end can use—everything."

Carmela's dark eyes widened. "What exactly is it?"

There was a pause, then Margot spoke. "I'm hoping to be a medical missionary."

Carmela and the other two remained silent, then Carmela spoke. "You do mean a missionary? Not just an ordinary doctor? But that means joining an Order, and you know what *that* means, Margot." She relapsed into her own language. "You may be sent anywhere—but anywhere in the world. You can never marry or have children of your own."

Margot nodded. "I know. I've thought of all that."

Len and Con waited for the next inevitable question, "Which Order?" It never came. Carmela's mind ran on other lines.

"How long have you thought of this?"

"Since I was a kid, actually. I think, looking back, that I've always wanted it, more or less. That is why I had such a bother with my devil—remember, you two?" She swung round on her sisters.

Carmela looked at them. "But did you know of this at all?"

"I knew it more or less," Len said. "No, Margot never told me. I just felt it in myself. I think Mamma did, too. What about you, Con?"

Con spoke slowly. "I've—wondered at times. Not way back in the past, but for the last year or two. But you said nothing, so—I couldn't butt in on you."

"Do your parents know?" Carmela asked.

"I've not actually told them—but I think they do—Mamma anyhow. She usually knows what we're thinking. But she wouldn't ask questions unless we wanted her to. What's private to us is private to us where she's concerned."

Len backed her up in this statement. "She knows. You've no idea how hard it is to keep a secret from her—a secret of that kind. But she never tries to drag things out of us."

Margot gave Carmela a straight look. "I suppose it had better come out now. I didn't want to talk of it before. I know you've all thought me very changeable and I admit I've dithered. It's such a tremendous thing. But I'm settled now. You see I didn't want to say anything definite until I could be quite certain. And don't you pity me because I shan't marry in the world, Carmela. For one thing I *shall* have children—patients and so on. And," she went on in lower tones, "I shall be married—though it won't be the sort of marriage the rest of you will have. And I'll have plenty of adventures, I expect. But you can see for yourself why I want to know so much. I shall do my medical course and when I've got my M.B. I hope to enter the Order of Blue Nuns and from there I shall go to the School of Tropical Nursing and work for my diploma in tropical medicines. After that—who knows?"

"I can scarcely believe it," Carmela said. "All the same, I can see you doing it," she went on. "Well, if that is what you want to do I hope you will be very happy in it."

"Thanks a lot," Margot said.

There was a slight pause, then Carmela heard her name called and went off while the Maynards stood together.

"You always were the adventurous one," Len said at last.

"What about you?" Margot demanded. "You're facing a big adventure, too, aren't you?"

Len flushed. "Nothing is settled and I don't know if it's what I shall finally want. Anyhow, I'm doing nothing until I've got my degree, that's flat."

Con chuckled. "Well, you'll have to reckon with Reg, my love. *He* knows what he wants, all right!"

Len shook her head. "He may, but I don't. It's something you've got to be very sure of. Anyhow, I want my degree before I settle to anything else. That means a wait of two if not three years. There's plenty of time to think it over."

"Poor Reg!" Con laughed.

"If he really wants you he'll be patient," Margot said, her blue eyes searching her elder sister's face. "But it's going to mean a few changes for him. However, I imagine he's thought of all that. Well, life looks like being interesting for all three of us in the not so very distant future. For I suppose you'll be settling down seriously to your writing, Con? What do you want to write in the main?"

"I don't exactly know. I think I'd like to pitch in on an historical novel, but it'll need a lot of thinking over. You can't just write any sort of yarn and embellish it with a few 'forsooths' and 'yea verilys'—not in these days. You've got to get all your data accurate and that means swotting up on your period in detail."

"Have you fixed on any period?" Len asked.

"Not yet. It needs thinking over as much as anything else. Have *you* any ideas on the subject?" She looked at her sisters with eager brown eyes.

"Well, as I've never given much thought to it, I haven't," Margot said. "What about you, Len?"

Len shook her head. "I know my favourite period, but it mightn't coincide with yours, Con. If I wanted to write a book I'd go tooth and nail for the time when Queen Victoria came to the throne. It must be frightfully interesting."

"Do you think so?" Con eyed her musingly. "But why?"

"Well, just think. She was a queen after a series of kings. The last three kings were all old men and now a young girl has come to the throne—she was only eighteen, wasn't she—and not very much was known about her. That would make it interesting for a start."

Margot glanced at her watch. "Caramba! I'll tell you something that is even more interesting at the present moment. It's nearly twenty-two hours and we ought to be indoors going to bed and not out here discussing history. Con, you'll have to leave the question for the moment but we'll return to it to-morrow. It's quite as absorbing a subject as either of ours. But if we stay here even five minutes longer, other people will be talking and in none too uncertain tones, either."

Len turned her wrist and gave an exclamation of horror. "Where has the time gone to? Come on, you two! Back to the house! Con, I'll think it over again. So will Margot and of course you will yourself. We'll discuss it in detail to-morrow. Meanwhile—" and she set the example by heading at full speed for the school. There were certain duties for both the Head Girl and the prefects to perform before they could go to bed and they had left themselves very little time to see to them.

They parted at the foot of the stairs, Len going to the study for a final word with the Head and the other two racing upstairs as quietly as possible to make their neglected dormitory rounds before retiring to their own beds. They went on tiptoe so as not to disturb any of the Juniors who might be light sleepers. As a result they nearly caught Jocelyn who was just opening the dormitory door to peer out to see if the lights were out on the stairs. Con had just turned the corner as Jocelyn turned the door handle and that young person had barely time to release the knob and scuttle back to her cubicle before the prefect did glance in to make sure that all was as it should be. Luckily for Jocelyn, Con was not over-observant and never noticed that one set of curtains was moving slightly. The only sound to be heard was of steady breathing. Con concluded that the entire dormitory was slumbering peacefully as it ought to be, and withdrew as noiselessly as she had come to attend to the others before slipping into her own where she undressed speedily and was soon sleeping the sleep of the justly weary.

Neither of the other two found anything to trouble them and soon all three were as sound asleep as most of the others. Not everyone, however, was slumbering. In certain dormitories were various young monkeys who had planned the daring feat of a midnight picnic, thanks to a parcel received by Carlotta von Eschenau earlier in the day. Normally it would have arrived at the office where Miss Dene would have handed it on to Matron to deal with; but on this occasion it had been brought by Carlotta's eldest brother, a gay youth of eighteen, who was taking a brief motoring holiday in Switzerland and had offered to save his parents money and trouble by taking the parcel and leaving it at the school. He had paid his youngest sister a brief visit, handing over the package during the course of it, and Carlotta had contrived to smuggle it upstairs to her cubicle together with a packet of underclothes which she religiously handed over to Matron. Of the tuck which Wolfgang had also brought she said nothing. She had managed to inform her own gang of it, however, and as there was little hope that they could conceal it for more than one day, the young sinners had resolved to fall in with Jocelyn's suggestion of a midnight picnic in the grounds that very night.

"It'll be something new to do," Jocelyn had pointed out, "and we can get out of one of the side-doors. But we'll have to wait until we can be sure that everyone else in the school is asleep," she added. "We'll go to bed as usual—"

"But that we must certainly do," Angelique Ste Barbe agreed.

Sandra Johnson giggled. "I should say so! Then when do we get out, Jos?"

"When I wake you," Jocelyn said. "Don't take off more of your clothes than you must and then you can just slip your frock over what you've got on and that will save time."

"It'll be safer, too," Barbara Craven pointed out. "Less chance of waking up the others, you see, but are *you* sure of waking up at the right time?"

"I'm sure all right. I can always wake myself when I want to. You needn't worry about that."

"That," remarked Anna Engels, "is quite true. Then we will leave that to you, Jocelyn."

Maureen O'Toole giggled. "Won't it be fun? And more exciting to have a picnic instead of just a midnight. I'll bet that's never been done before in this school."

There was no one to tell her that it had been done many years ago when the school was on St Briavel's Island off the Pembrokeshire coast. The instigators of that feast were still at the school, though Priscilla Dawbarn was now an important prefect and Prudence, who had always been a firebrand, had sobered down during this past year or so and had become very much more responsible than anyone had ever expected she would. Both were leaving at the end of the term along with quite a number of the other Seniors and neither would have been grateful to anyone who had resurrected that old story of their past misdoings. It was just as well that none of the Middles knew much about the episode.

In fact the talk had to cease just then as the bell rang for the end of the break and they had to go back to their lessons; but they met at intervals during the day to work out sundry details of their proposed picnic and when they went to bed they were all agog, though they were careful to cover up their feelings as much as they could.

Jocelyn slept in Wisteria dormitory and no other member of her crowd was there, but Barbara and two Swiss girls—Anna and Angelique—were next door in Marguerite; Sandra and Maureen were in Daffodil in the middle of the corridor; Carlotta was next door in Heather; Ottillie right at the far end in Edelweiss. Jocelyn for once showed caution and waited fully twenty minutes before she finally set off on her journey to Ottillie. She wore her dressing-gown over her frock and she thought that if anyone caught her she could always make the excuse that she wanted a drink of water. Goodness knew it was hot enough!

And at that moment she suddenly remembered that none of them had thought of drinks. What were they to do about that? Jocelyn forgot all about the caution which had so far brought her safely through any risks. She swung round and headed for the bathrooms. If nothing else they must have water. She did retain enough sense to go quietly, but that was about all. She didn't even think how she was to carry the water when she got it and the bathroom glass would hardly hold enough to satisfy eight girls.

Unluckily for her, Jack Lambert had wakened up a few minutes earlier with a raging thirst and she had decided that she could not exist a moment longer without a drink of water. She had never noticed Jocelyn at the far end of the corridor and when that young woman came hurtling down to the bathroom and tried to wrench the door open, it was just as Jack, having quenched her thirst, tried to open it from the other side. The result was that the door knob, which never had gentle treatment, gave way in Jack's hand, and Jack was left shut into the bathroom with no means of escape until someone attended to the knob from the outside, while Jocelyn lost her head, fled back to her own abode and left Jack to her fate.

"Who's the idiot out there? Shove the shank back and let me out!" Jack demanded furiously.

She got no reply though she repeated her commands several times—in fact until it dawned on her that no one was there. Then her annoyance changed to consternation. Was she stuck in the bathroom until morning?

"Not me," she muttered as she laid the useless knob in the toilet basin. "All the same I don't want to create a scene. I *could* yell my head off and someone would hear and come to inquire, but that would mean waking up the whole house. I don't want to do that if it can be avoided. Matey at least would have plenty to say! What about climbing out into the garden?"

She went to the window, pushed the lattice open and gazed down hopefully on the flower-border below. There was no help to be found there. The walls were smooth and even, without any cracks which would help if she tried to climb down. Neither was there a down-runner pipe which would have made things easy.

"And then!" ruminated Jack, "even if I get down how am I to get back into the house? There may be an unlocked door or window, but it's not awfully likely. I don't want to rouse the house, quite apart from the fact that whoever was on the other side might get into a row. And that, unless I'm badly mistaken, is most likely to happen. If it had been someone wanting a drink like me, why should she have scrammed as she did? I'll bet it's some kid on an unlawful occasion. All the same, I don't propose to spend the night here—not with exams beginning to-morrow. Oh, *drat* the little ass, whoever she is! Why did she have to scram like that?"

She went back to the window and leaned out. "I wonder if I could hang by my hands and drop? It's not so very much of a drop after all and I do know how to do it scientifically. I might bump myself a bit, but not to hurt badly. Shall I have a go?" She stared down, then she shook her head. "Better not, perhaps. Matey may make a fuss if I rouse the house, but she'd make far more of a fuss if I damaged an ankle or so. Oh *bother* whoever it was! Why didn't the silly kid shove the handle back?"

She drew in her head and sat down on the edge of the bath. "Here's a pretty kettle of fish! It looks as if I'll either have to bed down here or rouse the place. But I *can't* bed down. I'll never sleep and the exams begin to-morrow! I want my sleep before I have to tackle geometry and Latin I. Oh bother—bother—*bother*!"

However, the choice seemed to lie between the two alternatives and very reluctantly she decided on the second one. After all, she had done nothing against rules. As for the partner in the accident to the door-handle, she must make her own explanation and take what was coming to her.

"And serve her jolly well right!" said Jack aloud viciously. "Well, here goes!" And she began to hammer on the door with her fists as hard as she could.

She got no results at first. What with the heat of the day and their exertions the girls were more or less asleep, except for the would-be picnickers, and they froze with horror as they heard the banging.

Barbara Craven plucked up courage to tumble out of bed and look out into the corridor, by which time Jack had begun to yell at the top of her voice, banging having proved ineffectual. That woke quite a number of people, including Matron Duffin of St Clare's, who promptly scrambled out of bed, pulled on her dressing-gown and emerged from her room on the landing above to listen as, with the memory of Barbara Henschell's accident, she knotted the cord of her dressing-gown firmly before descending to find out what was happening below. By this time quite half the house was astir and various doors were opening, including Con Maynard's. Con, in fact, rudely roused from a sweet sleep, forgot about either bedroom slippers or dressing-gown and shot out just as she was in her pyjamas.

She found a surging mass of girls in the corridor, all asking what was happening and others hurrying to join them. She also nearly fell into Matron Duffin's arms and just checked herself in time.

"Sorry, Matron!" she gasped. "I didn't hurt you, did I?"

"Never mind me! Help me to calm this riot at once!" Matron said abruptly.

Con turned on the turbulent crew about her while Matron went into the short bathroom corridor to find out who had caused the first disturbance. "Stop that row and back to your dormitories, every one of you!" she commanded in a stentorian voice which helped to calm them considerably. "Do you want to wake the whole place? Back, I say! And be quiet at once!"

They went more from sheer astonishment than anything else. Con had always been the quietest of the triplets and no one had had any idea that she could yell like that, much less glare round them with a look that Matey herself could scarcely have bettered. Sheepishly they began to return to their cubicles and by the time that Matron Duffin had discovered that the door into A bathroom was handleless in every sense of the word since Jocelyn, in the shock of it all, had gone off with the shank which was now lying under her bed, the dormitories were more or less in their usual order.

"Who is in there?" Matron demanded when she could make herself heard by the prisoner.

"Me—Jack Lambert," Jack replied.

"What are you doing there at this time? But never mind that for the moment. How did this happen? Is the shank on your side?"

"No; only the knob," Jack replied meekly. "I can't do a thing about it."

"I see. Well, you'll have to be patient for a little. One mercy, you can't be cold on a night like this. Sit down and wait a little and we'll soon set you free. Though just how is beyond me at the moment!" Matron added, talking to herself rather than to Jack. "I suppose we must get Gaudenz to bring his tools and that means dressing and going across to his place. H'm! This isn't going to be very quick work." She spoke to Jack again. "Tell me, Jack, how it happened."

"I woke up as dry as the Sahara," Jack said, "and I came to get a drink of water. Then, when I wanted to come back and turned the knob there was someone on the other side and—well, between us we wrenched it, I suppose, and I was left with this side knob in my hand and whoever it was must have been scared for she vamoosed. Didn't she leave the other bit on the floor?"

112

"Nothing here," Matron said after a sweeping look round. "She must have taken it with her. You didn't get any idea who it was, did you?"

"Not I. I heard her going off at the rate of no man's business, but *who* it was I haven't the foggiest. Some kid or other, I should think."

"I see. Well, make yourself as comfortable as you can until I get back. I won't be any longer than I can help."

"Thank you Matron." Jack had pulled herself together by this time although inwardly she was raging. A nice preparation this for the exams!

"I'm just going," Matron said. "And here's Con Maynard so I'll leave her to talk to you till I get back with Gaudenz. Con, you stay and cheer Jack up, will you? I'll be as quick as I can, but it means fetching Gaudenz and his tools."

"But there are tools in the hobbies cupboard," Con said. "What will you want?"

Matron's face brightened. "So there are! Let me see. Oh, I think if we could get something that would act as the shank, Jack could fix her knob on it and she could turn it. I'm glad you thought of that, Con. Oh, are the girls all in bed?"

"I've been making the rounds," Con said, "and when we've set poor Jack free may I come to your room? I've something to show you."

Matron glanced at her. "Have you, indeed! Yes, by all means come. Jack, we should be able to free you in a few minutes. Be patient a little longer."

"I'm O.K.," said Jack as nonchalantly as she could. "But I *would* like to get to my bed and to sleep. Goodness knows what my Latin paper will be like after all this."

"Don't worry. Dr Benson shall have this explained to her in full."

"Well, that's all right. And thank goodness it's just end-of-term exams and not a public exam!" Jack said in heartfelt tones. Suddenly she giggled. "Now if only I'd had my towels with me I could have had a bath—but I haven't."

But Matron had departed, first to her room for a tape measure to get some idea of the width required for a shank, and then down to the hobbies cupboard in search of something that would serve their purpose. She was speedily back with half a dozen oddments and after careful trial one was found that would slide through. Jack fixed the knob on the end, she turned it and at last she was free.

Matron sent Con back to her own dormitory before escorting the victim to hers and tucking her in with a glass of water beside her, and then she retired to her own bed after fixing a label on the bathroom door on which was printed "Out of Order". It would be time enough in the morning to rearrange the bath lists and she was tired out. But this must be reported to the Head and she could sort it out.

As for what Con had wanted to see her about, she had refused to listen to anything. "You can come to me as soon as you like in the morning, but it's more than time we were both asleep," she had said firmly.

And Con had departed, nothing loath. She could scarcely keep her eyes open by this time.

Chapter IX

CONSEQUENCES

MATRON Duffin was stripping her bed when Con tapped at her door early next morning.

She called out, "Come in!" but when she saw Con, she exclaimed. "Con! I never expected you to be up so early after our broken night. How do you feel? Are you very tired? And what on earth is that parcel under your arm?"

Con laid the bulky parcel on the table by the window. "That's what I thought you'd better find out, Matron. It was on the floor in Heather and I found it when I went the rounds after we sent the rabble to bed." She spoke in easy, fluent French. "My own idea is that it is contraband, but to whom it belongs or what it was doing there, I cannot say."

"We'll soon find out." Matron's reply was also in French which was the language for the day. "Hand me the scissors from my work-basket, please."

Con produced a big pair of cutting-out scissors and Matron snipped the string which tied up the parcel. It was the work of a moment to strip off string and paper and lay bare a small carton. Matron opened that and proceeded to empty it. It contained a box of sweets, another of preserved ginger, two packets of biscuits and another of jumbles; at the bottom was a large cake. Matron spread them out and eyed them balefully.

"Somebody was evidently going to enjoy a feast—several somebodies, in fact," she said, relapsing into her own tongue. "Where did these come from, I wonder? And how were they smuggled in? For they certainly did not come by post. Miss

Dene would have handed them to me in that case …"

Con thought. "Didn't someone have a visitor yesterday? Now who was it?"

"Carlotta von Eschenau. Her brother Wolfgang. He must have brought it."

"Then," said Con with deep conviction, "we don't need to ask who were her partners in crime. That crew hang together like a bunch of grapes."

Matron bundled the things back into the carton. "Carlotta, certainly. We must ask the others, of course, before we make sure. But I think you're right, Con. Then now we also know who was responsible for the door handle. I must think this over. Thank you, Con. Say nothing to anyone for the moment, but I rather think this must be reported to the Head. But what were they thinking of?"

"A midnight," Con said with a giggle. "Silly little idiots! They would almost certainly have been caught out. They're nearly all in different dormitories. Let's see." She thought it over. Then she looked at Matron. "I suppose they meant to feed in Heather. But which of them was messing about with the bathroom—and why?"

Matron laughed. "That's easy enough. They wanted drinks so someone went to the bathroom for water as there was nothing else to be had." She picked up the carton, and pushed it into a cupboard. "Thank you, Con. I'll inquire into the matter after Frühstück unless I decide that it had better go straight to Miss Annersley."

"There'll be a frightful row if you decide that way," Con said thoughtfully.

"Serve them right!" Matron retorted briskly. "If that was the idea then they were breaking rules by the dozen and well they knew it! No, Con; I can't possibly pass over anything as blatant as midnighting. If I think I should deal with it myself, I probably shall; but I'm not at all sure. Now, my dear, I must turn you out as I have any amount to do. By the way, say nothing about this affair to the others for the moment."

"No, Matron." Con left the room and went off for 'cello practice before Frühstück. But she felt rather sorry for the sinners if they had to be reported. Meanwhile, in Heather, Carlotta was realising that her contraband had vanished and was filled with consternation. Where had it gone? Who had taken it? Did Matron know about it? In that case there would be trouble. What should she do? The only idea that occurred to her was to get hold of Jocelyn as quickly as possible and see what she suggested. But if it was Matron who had taken the parcel away Carlotta could not see what they could do about it.

"Oh, I wish I had taken it to Matron first of all!" she thought.

Other people were feeling the same way though mostly without the big reason that Carlotta had. They had no idea what had caused the noise during the night, but they felt somehow that it would not be long before Matron or one of the prefects would connect them with it.

They dressed, stripped their beds, and then were all set to race downstairs and have a hasty conference, but the gong sounded for Frühstück and they had to give up that idea. The result was that they were unable to do anything about it at once, for after the meal they had to go and make their beds and tidy their cubicles and after that came a morning walk.

There was little hope of a conference before Prayers and they knew it, but Carlotta did contrive to get hold of Jocelyn for about two minutes and tell her that her tuck had vanished, whereat Jocelyn whistled expressively.

"And I've got that doorhandle," she confided in return. "I must get it back somehow."

There was no time for more. The bell sounded and they had to go to their formrooms to collect their needs for the morning.

Not many, these, since it was exam week. They would have talked together then, but their form mistress, Miss Carey, was before them, so they had to let it alone for the moment. They took their pens, pencils, rulers and indiarubbers and that was all they would need. Then Miss Carey marched them out to the garden and to one of the big trestle tables where there were big sheets of blotting paper with a name on each sheet.

"Find your places," Miss Carey said, "and leave your pens, etc., on top of the blotting paper, ready for when you come back. Did you bring your hymn-books? Why not? You knew you would need them. *One* girl go back and collect them and bring them here. Ottillie, you go. Be quick, please!"

Ottillie hurried off and Miss Carey, who had sensed the uneasy atmosphere among the crowd, stood watching them meditatively in a way that made those people with unhappy consciences most uncomfortable.

"Oh dear!" the mistress said to herself. "What have they been up to now, I wonder?" She was to learn all too soon.

Ottillie came back with the hymnbooks and they were distributed. The first bell rang for register and they had to go and stand in their places while Miss Carey called the roll. That done, she mustered them into double lines and marched them off, the Protestant girls to the Speisesaal and the Catholics to the Gym where Prayers must be taken for the full exam week. Having done this, she summoned a passing prefect to take charge while she hurried to the staffroom to collect her requirements for the morning and relax with her confreres for a few moments.

"What's the matter with you, Beth?" demanded Nancy Wilmot. "You look as if the heavens might drop on you at any moment. Not feeling ill, are you?"

"No, but expecting trouble at any moment," Beth Carey told her.

"Good gracious! Why on earth?"

"There's something up with my form—or some of them, anyhow."

"Which ones?" Kathy Ferrars asked.

"Need you ask? The usual crew, of course. Oh, I expect I'll know all about it before long. But if it's they who were responsible for last night's riot I'll feel like doing murder. The night before the exams, if you please! The Head will be furious."

"She won't blame you, though," Nancy said soothingly. "Cheer up! At least they won't get into much mischief today with exams. By the way, warn them to be quiet at Break, will you? The senior geometry exam won't be finished by that time, and judging by what I know of those papers they'll need every moment of their time."

"I'll warn and double warn them!" Beth Carey said viciously.

"Good! And there goes the bell for Prayers. Avant, mes amies. We mustn't set the little dears a bad example whatever else we do."

The mistresses went off down the wide front stairs in groups of threes and fours, entered the Speisesaal by the big double doors at the top end of the room, and took their places round the high table which was theirs by prescriptive right. Miss Lawrence, Head of the Music staff, went to the little upright piano set across a corner and began to play softly. The Head came in a minute or two later and Prayers began.

During them the sinners in the Speisesaal began to cheer up a little. Perhaps it was all right so far as Miss Annersley was concerned. Perhaps there had been no report to her and Matron meant to deal with it herself. That would be bad enough. Matron Duffin was liked by everyone, but she could be strict enough when she chose. She would certainly have plenty to say if she knew or guessed about the midnighting business. And equally certain she would punish such a thing pretty sharply. When they rose from their knees, however, they were feeling happier.

"Sit, please, girls," Miss Annersley said. "As soon as the rest of the girls join us I have something to say to all of you."

They didn't have to wait long. Almost at once the rest of the girls came in and took their places, while the Catholic members of the staff went to their places at the high table. Every eye was now glued to the high table, though the majority of the girls fancied they were only going to be given the usual warning about being quiet during this week for the sake of the exam girls. There was not only themselves to consider, but the girls from St Hilda's, another school about three or four miles away at Ste Cecilie who always came to the Chalet School to sit for the public exams. In fact they could now hear the horn of the school bus bringing the dozen or so people and the mistress in charge. Miss Annersley could hear it, too, but she paid no heed. Jocelyn and her gang looked at her and their hearts sank. She stood tall and stately at the front of the dais and there was a grim look about her mouth which told them all too plainly that what she had to say was likely to be unpleasant.

"First," she said, "I am warning you younger ones that for this week and two days of next you must all be quiet if you are near the house. Remember that the public exams will be going on and people who are sitting for them don't want to be disturbed by wild shrieks. Is that understood?"

"Yes, Miss Annersley," a chorus from the girls.

"Good. I wish I could stop there," she went on gravely, "but unfortunately I cannot. Carlotta von Eschenau, is this yours?" She held up the fatal carton which had been on the table beside her.

"Oui, Madame," Carlotta whispered.

"Your brother brought it yesterday when he visited you?"

"Oui, Madame." Carlotta was crimson and she could hardly get the words out.

"Come out, please." Carlotta left her place and literally crawled up to the dais where she stood twisting her hands together.

"Tell me, why did you not take it straight to Matron after he had gone?"

There was no reply. The Head looked at her severely. "You know the rule, do you not? Then why did you not take it to Matron? Answer me, please."

"I—I—" That was as far as Carlotta got. She was biting her lip and tears were not far away. The Head knew it and she gave the child a moment's respite to pull herself together. Then she spoke again.

"Furthermore, I do not believe that you did this alone." She turned to the others. "Those girls who knew about this, please stand up."

The others rose, most of them reluctantly, though Jocelyn literally bounced to her feet, defiance in her look. The Head looked from one to another. "I see. In that case the rest may go and prepare for work. No; one moment. Was anyone out of her cubicle last night before you were all roused?"

No one had been as it chanced, so the Head nodded to Miss Lawrence who sat down at the piano and broke into a stately march and they all marched off, leaving the eight still standing and all looking very hangdog. The mistresses went off with the school and when the last had gone the Head spoke again—in her very iciest tones. "You eight little girls form into line and go to my study—and in silence, please. No one is to speak."

Dumbly they obeyed her. Even if they had wanted to they had little chance of talking. The Head had handed her books to the nearest mistress to return to the study. Miss Andrews was about to leave when the eight appeared and she drew back and waited with them until the Head arrived.

"Thank you, Miss Andrews," Miss Annersley said with a quick smile.

Miss Andrews went out and the Head was left with the culprits.

"You may sit down," she said, still in that very chilly tone. "Over there on the couch and the ottoman."

"Oh, *crumbs*!" Jocelyn said inwardly. "We're for it this time!"

They sat down very primly, feet and knees together, hands folded in their laps.

"Now," said the Head, "I want the whole of this story—the whole of it, if you please, and don't let me have to drag it out of you word by word. Begin, please, Carlotta, since the first fault seems to have been yours. Your brother brought you this parcel and instead of taking it straight to Matron as you very well knew you ought, you hid it. Where, if you please?"

"Under—under my bed," Carlotta faltered.

"I see, and what did you propose to do with the contents?"

"I—we—"

Carlotta stopped there and Jocelyn took up the tale. "Please, we were going to have a—a picnic in the garden."

"You were *what*?" Miss Annersley almost gasped.

"Have a—a picnic—in the garden," Jocelyn faltered, almost overcome by the glare she was receiving.

The Head said nothing for a full minute. Then she glanced along the line of girls and there was nothing friendly in her glance. It was too much and at least three of them burst into tears.

"Stop crying," Miss Annersley said severely. "Let me understand this. You were proposing to go out into the grounds at that hour? How did you expect to get out of the house?"

Jocelyn wriggled uncomfortably. This was something she had hoped need not come out. Still, she had been asked the question and she was nothing if not truthful.

"Please, I rubbed the bolts with some of the butter from Abendessen—s-so that they wouldn't m-make a noise."

"Nothing if not ingenious," the Head said to herself. Aloud she said, "So, not content with breaking at least three strict rules you wasted good food. Jocelyn, I am ashamed of you!"

"It—it was only a little bit," Jocelyn mumbled. "And I took it from my own pats."

"That makes it no better."

Jocelyn bit her lips. In another moment she must cry as her weaker confreres were doing and she had a boyish scorn for tears. There was only one thing she could do to avoid it. Setting her feet firmly and gripping her hands together, she summoned up all her courage. "Well, it was all I could get!"

Miss Annersley looked at her thoughtfully. "I see. Well; go on. You did not manage to get out, of course. Did you have anything to do with the breaking of the handle of the bathroom door?"

"Y-yes."

"Tell me all about it, please." The Head spoke blandly, but her blandness was no comfort to the eight. There was a certain something about it that warned them there was much more to come.

Jocelyn gripped her fingers together even more tightly. Then she spoke. "I—I suddenly remembered that—that we had nothing to drink so I—I went to the bathroom to get some water. I—I thought it would be—be—b-better than nothing." She stopped short.

"I see. And how far did you imagine one tumbler of water would go among you all?"

"I—I didn't think of that."

"I see. Did you think at all?"

"I—I—no," Jocelyn confessed.

"So I imagine. Well; continue. What happened?"

"Someone else was in the bathroom and when she turned the handle I was just turning it, too, and I tugged and—and it came away in my hand and then, well, I didn't know what to do so I just—went back to the dormitory and then someone began to yell and—and I forgot all about it, and—and that's all."

"What did you do with the handle?"

"W-well, I—I took it with me. I put it under my bed, but when I l-looked for it this morning it—it wasn't—wasn't there. I d-don't know where it is now."

It was taking Jocelyn all her time to control herself now.

Carlotta suddenly nerved herself to come to her leader's rescue. "Please, Miss Annersley," she said in her own language, "Don't blame it all on Jocelyn. I know," she swallowed hard, "if I had given that parcel to Matron this would not have happened, b-but—" There she broke off, unable to go any further.

The Head nodded. "Quite so. Yours was the first wrongdoing of all, Carlotta. You know the rule about tuck, but you chose to break it deliberately. And what about you others? You know the rule, too. Did you try to stop Carlotta and Jocelyn or did you fall in with their plans without saying a word?"

A murmur of assent arose, not unmixed with sobs from the weaker members of the crew. Miss Annersley nodded and leaned back in her chair.

"I see! In fact, you none of you thought for yourselves. You were satisfied to follow Jocelyn and Carlotta blindfold. Right! Well, we can't have that sort of thing going on, especially in girls of your age. In less than three years you should all be seniors and we don't like seniors who are as weak-kneed as all that. You must learn to stand on your own feet, and make your own decisions. Therefore," she spoke very weightily, "for the next week you will not be allowed to be together, either in the dormitories or in formrooms. During free times you will be allotted to various other forms. Carlotta, your parcel will be added to one that we are sending to Innsbruck. Jocelyn, you will pay one-half of the repair to the door-handle which will, I am afraid, dip into your pocket-money. The rest of you will go to get your writing materials, rulers and so on and come back here. Jocelyn, ring that bell, please."

Jocelyn went to ring the bell. The other girls did their best to pull themselves together and the Head watched them gravely until one of the maids came. Marie received orders to bring Len Maynard and went off. When she had gone, the Head turned to her culprits again.

"I have one more thing to say. You realize, I hope, that I might well have forbidden you the Sale? I have not done so, but I warn you all to be very careful because if you break rules any further this week or are sent to me for any trouble, that is what I shall do. I will not permit this flagrant flouting of school rules. Ah, here is Len. Len, a word with you. You children may go into the corridor and wait there."

Len came in, looking very grave and very much the Head Girl. Before her steady gaze the sinners shrank back and made themselves as small as possible as they filed past her out into the corridor. When the door closed on Jocelyn the Head turned to Len and gave a brief explanation.

"I'm sorry, but I'm afraid I must move some of you seniors, but it's only for a week or so. It was a choice between that and forbidding this lot the Sale and I don't want to do that. But punished they must be and in such a way that they won't forget it in a hurry. Will you bring Con and Margot, and Ted, Ruey and Carmela, Eve and Jeanne Daudet. Share the eight out among you and see to their changing dormitories. I'll come along later and arrange for their change of forms. Luckily they'll be doing exams for the moment, and that will part them all adequately at present. Now run along, dear. Leave them each in a separate room while you explain to the others. Then you can send them to the exam tables and that will settle them for the time being."

Len nodded and went off and the result was that the eight reprobates found themselves well and truly separated and faced with exams for which they felt far from ready. In fact their exam papers brought down their exam totals most shockingly, and when

125

their reports arrived at home they had to answer some difficult questions.

What was even worse was the fact that their prefect caretakers watched them closely and saw to it that they had no chance to condole with each other. As for Jocelyn, the added punishment of being short of cash just before the Sale made her think rather more deeply than she had done before. Jack Lambert, paying her share of the damage for the door, regretted that she had been so rough with the handle, though she could afford the loss better than Jocelyn.

But one thing was certain. It would be a long time before anyone thought of midnighting again. Miss Annersley's prompt action had seen to that.

Chapter X

MINETTE'S SURPRISE

"WELL, at least we can hope for a little peace for the next few days." Thus said Ted Grantley during Break that same morning. "Most folk will be up to the eyes mentally in the exams and I should judge from all I can see that the Head must have been at her most crushing with that octet. Where, by the way, did they propose to celebrate their midnight?"

Len giggled wholeheartedly. "That's the cream of it! Believe it or not they meant to hold a midnight picnic in the garden!"

"What!" The cry came from half a dozen people.

"Well, I suppose there's nothing like being original," Carmela commented. "I'm sure that's never been done in this school before."

"That's where you're wrong," Con said. She looked at her sisters and laughed. "When we were on St Briavel's Island a bunch of Middles got the same idea. What's more, they did get out, but someone had turned pigs into the orchard where the party was to be held and they fell over them, which annoyed the old mother and she went for them."

"One can hardly blame her," Marie Hüber said seriously. "If they trampled on one of her babies she would be very angry, nicht wahr?"

"From all accounts she was raging," Margot said. "Of course it was much easier for them than the present crowd. For one thing they were all in the same dormy. For another, Matey was tied up with Julie Lucy. You remember Julie had that awful go of peritonitis the term before. She was seized with a bad attack of hiccoughs at bedtime and Matey dared not leave her. Otherwise I doubt if anyone could have got out to the orchard without being well and truly caught."

"What was the end of it?" Carmela asked with interest.

"They all ran for it and either scrambled through or over the hedge—"

"You're out there," interrupted Priscilla Dawbarn, who had been listening to the account with very pink cheeks. "We made for the gate and got over somehow."

"*You?* Do you mean you were in it?" Eve Hurrell demanded.

"Alas for the sins of my youth!" Priscilla retorted. "Both Prue and I were up to the neck in it. Come off it, Eve! You know we were never little angels in those days."

She laughed as she went on, "Well, we got all that was coming to us, I can assure you. The Head wiped up the floor with us. We were moved into other dormies. We were cut out of all form picnics and we weren't allowed to compete in the Regatta which was almost on top of us. It was exams, and the Head had taken at least twenty minutes of the exam time, telling us what she thought of us. She made us go with her to the village to fill in what was left of the time and we had to do our exams after—tea, I suppose it would be in those days. We thought Miss Annersley horribly hard on us, but actually I see now that she let us down pretty lightly. All the same, no one thought of midnighting for a jolly long time after that."

Con laughed. "So I should imagine. Well, let's hope what she's done about Jocelyn and Co will hold them for the moment— little pests!"

"My dear, do you need to doubt that? Did you not see their faces when the Head sent them to her study?" Maria Zinkel asked impressively.

Margot laughed. "I saw them when Len was marching them off to begin their exams after the Head had finished with them.

They all looked as if the world had come to an end. If the Head had been telling them just what she thought of them that accounts for it. She has a tongue like a file on occasion."

"Well, she has forbidden them to see each other," observed Louise Grunbaum, "and she has given them one each in charge to us."

"Yes; and very annoying it is," Primrose Trevoase grumbled.

"And I'll tell you another annoying thing and that is that our bathroom is out of order," Ted said. "I only just managed to splash in, splash out this morning, and I do like to start the day feeling fresh after a bath. But our crowd has to share with people from Wistaria and Pansy and Narcissus and it was a regular scramble. I would like to know who's been doing what to that door."

"Oh, my dear girl! Have you never *seen* how some of those youngsters treat doors? Well, it will be attended to at once you may be sure. Luckily Gaudenz knows all about that sort of thing."

Margot looked round, for the Middles were beginning to come out into the garden and each prefect in charge of a sinner must claim her and keep her until the bell rang for the end of Break. The other people similarly burdened followed Margot's example and as the Middles appeared each prefect claimed her special charge and carried her off. They were none too pleased about it. It meant that they had little opportunity for a private chat. Result: none was exactly welcoming and their manner told their juniors that. It was not consoling to the already miserable octet, for even Jocelyn was affected by the general air of disapproval with which they were surrounded. In fact they were thankful when the bell rang for the end of Break and they were escorted back to their places at the exam tables where the people invigilating were awaiting them.

It went on like that for the whole day. In the Speisesaal they sat beside their guards. During the rest period they had to put their deck chairs alongside the same people. The afternoon's work began with an hour's revision and continued with games, during which they played Beanbags sitting in the shade of a tall pine with Miss Burnett in charge, while the rest made the most of their chances on the tennis courts. Games ended, the others were set free to amuse themselves quietly, but the eight were summoned to a shady corner of the garden where Matron set them to hem dusters while she read aloud to them from a travel book which interested none of them very much.

And so it went on for the whole day until by the time the bell sounded for bed they were thankful to hear it. "Bored" doesn't begin to describe their feelings. What was almost as bad was the feeling of deep disapproval which met them on every side.

"I wish," said Jocelyn aloud to herself, "that they used a cane in this school. It stings you up at the time, but at least it's over quickly and done with. This sort of thing is awful."

"To whom were you speaking?" asked Len who was escorting her to her new dormitory.

"To myself," Jocelyn returned with the beginning of defiance in her voice.

"Oh, I shouldn't do that," Len said suavely. "In any case corporal punishment has never been used in this school and it is most unlikely it ever will be. I'm afraid you'll have to put up with present conditions, boring or not."

Jocelyn had no more to say. Besides, by this time they had reached her new dormitory and she saw with dismay that it was a senior dormitory. Furthermore, it was only two doors away from Matron's room and Matron was reputed to sleep with one ear open. Jocelyn would be prohibited from even visiting if she felt like it. Not that she did just then. She was in trouble enough already.

Len ushered her into her cubicle and sat down on the window-sill. "Undress," she said briefly. "You wash in bathroom seven, cubicle four. I'll take you along when you're ready. Be quick."

Jocelyn was quick. Much later on when she and the others were able to meet and discuss things together again they discovered that they had all received the same treatment. Furthermore, they were all agreed that a more boring time they had never experienced.

"It was an *unsweetened rice pudding* of a time," Jocelyn gave it a name which took the fancy of the entire school and passed into Chalet School vocabulary as a permanency. But at least it did its work. The next few weeks were peaceful for the Chalet School.

This is not to say that the school was free of trouble. As Con Maynard said so far as she could trace there had never been a single term free from excitement from one cause or another. Len Maynard questioned her mother and Mrs Maynard had to own that she could not think of it ever happening.

"And if *she* doesn't know, no one else will," Margot said. "Oh well, it's quite pleasant for a change. Is that your history paper? Can I have a dekko, someone?"

Lesley Anderson obliged with a copy of the history paper and the prefects let the subject of the peace or otherwise of the School drop for the moment.

Things eased up a little next day when the eight were permitted to join the ordinary walk, but it didn't help matters very much, because Lower IV felt that the sinners had brought the form into a most unpleasant kind of limelight and were consequently sniffy with them. In short, even Jocelyn and Carlotta, who had begun by trying to appear casual about it, ended by being most miserable.

But when the week came to an end, Minette created a sensation by producing a litter of seven kittens! What was more the whole seven were toms! It caused a sensation not only in the Chalet School but at St Hilda's, the companion school which was flourishing in Ste Cecilie, the little village some three miles or so to the west. St Hilda's also owned a Minette who had so far never produced a larger litter than three. The Minette Surprise, as Jack Lambert called it, helped to smooth over the other matter and by the time the second week after the picnic that didn't come off had ended, Miss Annersley had decided that the punishment had been sufficiently severe and rescinded what might have been left.

The Sale was the next excitement, and people were beginning to sort out sundry objects for discussion as to whether they were good enough for raffles or must be priced and sold in the ordinary way.

On the whole, this was not a very difficult business. Anything about which it seemed likely there would be controversy was set aside for the staff to make the decision, but after that there came the final inspection of dresses.

Considering how much had been destroyed in the fire earlier in the term, things weren't too bad. The Four Seasons each had a background colour. For example, Spring was green, Summer was pink, Autumn was yellow and dark red, and Winter was scarlet and green. The prefects in charge of these different divisions wore loose robes in these colours. The typical people representing the divisions were John Peel for Autumn, Santa Claus for Winter, May Queen for Spring and Golden Wheat for Summer.

The very small folk would be flowers, butterflies, birds and so on, and their dresses were largely made of crepe paper. Quite a number were safe because the Juniors had been sent home in their costumes. There had been several which had to be renewed, but on the whole the Lower School hadn't come off so badly. It was the Senior Middles and the Middles who had to be fitted out from scratch. However, by the time the exams had come to an end, most of the missing dresses had been replaced adequately.

Finally on the Friday evening Miss Annersley organized a full-dress parade in Hall, when the girls marched round to be inspected by the staff.

"On the whole," said the Head after scrutinizing them closely,

"I think we may congratulate ourselves on the results of our hard labour. The dresses will do beautifully, and if we *are* short in one or two ways we have to remember that what we have lost was the collection of years. Now here are slips with your names. Pin your slip inside your dress and fold everything neatly; take your dress up to your dormitory and put it safely inside one of your drawers and shut the drawer. Remember that if anything happens to this lot, it isn't going to be easy to replace. You must take the greatest care. Now I think that is all I have to say for the moment, and I hope we shall have a very satisfactory Sale in spite of all our difficulties. Prefects, please escort the Juniors and Middles upstairs and see that they put their dresses away safely. The Seniors can look after themselves."

On the following Monday the girls began to sort out the goods to go on the various stalls. "I wish we could stick to our groups," Len said as she piled up the books for the bookstall. "I should like to stay with the books the whole time ... Oh, never tell me that that is a copy of *Tomakin and the Golden Jujubes*! I'm snaffling this if nobody objects. My copy had to be destroyed when we had chicken pox—remember?—and I've never been able to get another copy until this minute."

Three or four more people found books they had wanted to renew, but even so there were several piles left which were very useful to fit in on the stall. At this point Con came strolling up, a pile of tea cloths on her arms.

"Look here," she said. "These are all more or less of the same value. Should we just put them on one list?"

"Can if you like," Len said. "It might save trouble."

"Right. Then that's what we'll do."

"And now the next thing," said Ted. "There's all this pile of jigsaw puzzles. Where do we put them? With the books or in a heap by themselves?"

"Oh, I think by themselves," Margot said thoughtfully. "That'll give a neat pile one corner of the stall, and they all have to be priced separately. You'd better see to that, Priscilla. And Carmela—there are all those strings of beads that seem to have come in from nowhere that I can tell. They've just arrived."

"And very nice, too," said Eve with a grin. "They're none of them valuable, are they? Or *are* they?" she added thoughtfully, picking up a string.

"Had we better get someone who knows on to them?" Primrose asked.

"Well, *myself* I think they are mainly just beads," Priscilla remarked. "Not worth more than a few francs. We might hang them up on a long bar. They'll appeal to the kids, anyhow."

"Right. Well, that's settled," Jeanne Daudet observed.

Primrose cocked her head on one side. "Good! Then shall we get cracking on this lot?"

"Well, it would be something attempted, something done," Con observed.

"Right. Then let's get down to it," Eve said.

By this time the Middles were also hard at it, carrying out various articles intended for the different stalls, and the rest of the morning and most of the afternoon were occupied by filling various stands and showing off the different goods to their best advantage.

Kaffee und Kuchen was followed by a stroll for everybody. Then came Prayers, and after that the Juniors and Junior Middles went to bed; tired after their strenuous work but very pleased with the result.

The next day after Prayers the people who were responsible for the choral singing met in Hall, where Mr Denny set to work on a strenuous rehearsal of the half-dozen or so choruses which filled-in between solos in the concert, which was to be one of the entertainments in the afternoon. Then he turned to the soloists, who ranged from the Maynard triplets to Samaris Davies, who had been promoted to a flute solo. The Juniors were doing action songs and the Senior Middles and Inter V were responsible for a group of country dances.

"Well, if it goes on being as hot as this," Miss Burnett said, "I don't see anybody feeling like dancing. Glory, what weather!" She mopped her face and then added plaintively, "Is there anything to drink anywhere?"

"Plenty of water in the Splashery," Primrose informed her with a grin.

"I should like some of Karen's lemonade. That's much better in weather like this."

"Well, what's the matter with asking Matron if we can have some lemonade?" Eve suggested. "I'm sure she would agree."

"My dear girl, we shall have elevenses in another half-hour," Margot remarked. "Can't you hang out till then?"

"I suppose so. Oh well! But it is so *blazing* hot!"

The sound of the school bell brought them all to Hall, where Matron was waiting to issue her orders. She stood on the dais with her colleagues ranged behind her.

"Please listen to me," she said impressively. "It is abnormally hot today. It is forbidden to go out of doors without a hat. All girls must lie down after Mittagessen for a siesta this afternoon in the dormitories, and stay there until the gong sounds."

There were no comments made. In fact Matey would have been shocked if there had been any, but the girls were not surprised. It was rarely that the weather was as hot as this but when it occurred the School took precautions.

"All the same," Jocelyn grumbled to Althea, when they were finally sent upstairs to the dormitories. "I must say I think it's the limit. We're getting no tennis, no cricket, and not even rambles. It can't be necessary to tie us up as much as all that."

"It may be all right for you," Carlotta said, "but for me I find it very hot. Très fatiguant."

"Moi aussi," sighed Anna Engles.

"I wonder," Samaris said, "if we could have an evening swim. It would be lovely if we could. And it certainly would be cooling."

Half a dozen voices joined in a chorus of agreement at this, but nothing had been said and they had to settle down attired merely in their dressing-gowns with the curtains drawn in all the dormitories. They might grumble, but between the heat and the work of that morning most of them dozed off happily and there was peace in the school till sixteen hours brought the gong which called them to sponge and dress for Kaffee und Kuchen. After this the school coaches arrived and they were borne off for a cool drive, which was something quite unexpected.

Chapter XI

PREPARATIONS GO AHEAD

IT had been decided that the Wednesday of that week should be
devoted to confectionery stalls. There would be two; one for
cakes, fancy bread twists and little scones, the other for bon-
bons, chocolates and sweets of every kind. The prefects divided
up into two parties, each claiming so many younger girls to help
with the work. The Middles were set to cutting up silver paper to
cover the sweets. Frau Mieders, the Domestic Science Mistress,
had a collection of confectionery recipes which were second to
none and the school prided itself on the sweets. The girls
themselves had contributed to the collection and there had been
suggestions that the School should publish its own Confectionery
Recipe Book.

Margot claimed the head of the cake stall, Con voted for
sweets, and Len was informed that she could be overseer to the
lot. "What does one infer from that?" she asked suspiciously when
her sisters unloaded this information on her.

"Well, it means that you will be responsible for everything
being in decent order," Margot said sweetly.

"Well, upon my word!" exclaimed her indignant sister. "What
next, I should like to know? Oh no, my loves! If you take charge
of a division, you take charge of it, and only come to me for
necessary advice or assistance."

"Don't be lazy," said Margot severely. "It's not much to do,
and *someone's* got to be at the head."

"And who," Con pointed out, "should that be but the Head
Girl?"

After some argument they finally got things settled. Some people were put in charge of the boiled sweets, a certain number were set to making chocolates and Mdlle de Lachennais came to proffer her expert advice on French chocolate.

Carmela Walther, who was clever at modelling, collected sundry of the most artistic and led them off to model marzipan into flowers and fruit which were then carried off on trays and set to dry in the big ovens in the kitchens, and it was here that the first mishap occurred.

Audrey Everett was very artistic and she undertook to oversee the colouring of the marzipan with the help of certain members of the Fifth forms.

"Be careful how you use those dyes," Frau Mieders warned Audrey. "Remember that a little goes a long way." Then she turned to speak to Ted Grantley, who had come to see her about the slicing of the candied peel which had to be cut into long thin strips for a very special cake, and thought no more of it. Audrey went off with the box containing the vegetable dyes and set to work.

"How are you going to arrange it?" Joan Dancey asked.

"Well, I think we'll divide up the marzipan into different blocks, one girl in charge of each block and each colour. That would be a beginning," Audrey said, "and of course when we come to the more elaborate concerns we must use the brushes. For example, what have you got there, Connie?"

Connie Winter glanced up. "Well, someone presented me with a bottle of green which I presume will act as a background. When that's done, then I shall refer to another colour. I've got pink here but I should also like some yellow. Audrey, what about a spot of yellow?"

"What always puzzles me," Primrose Trevoase observed, "is why they never seem to have blue dyes."

"Yes, it's puzzled me," Yvette Olivier remarked. "I wonder what's the why of it?"

138

"Well, let's begin and not just talk," Priscilla Dawbarn said.

"Right. Pass me some of those little paint saucers along and I'll tip some of this green stuff into them and then we can begin."

The saucers were duly passed along and filled, the brushes used for the painting with the dye handed out, and then it happened. Eve, leaning across the table, slipped and went full length on top of the saucers, sending them flying in all directions. Most of the dye was deposited on the exclaiming girls, but one little saucer turned completely upside down and, caught by the flying hand of Carmela, lifted up and came neatly down on top of the bright head of Margot, who happened to be passing at the time.

There was a breathless silence for a moment and then Margot gave tongue in no uncertain manner. "What on earth do you think you're doing? Get me a towel, someone!"

Half a dozen people hurriedly grabbed the nearest kitchen towels and pressed them on her. She mopped up the green dye from her hair and Melanie Lucas, of VIb, surveying her own towel, was moved to wonder aloud if the dye was fast.

"For you know," she said seriously, to a little group of her own congeners, "it would look rather awful if someone had to turn up with green hair."

Margot cast one look of horror at her. "That's a nice thought," she said. "Really! What will you suggest next, Melanie?"

"Well," said Melanie apologetically, "I was just remembering what Auntie Joey told us happened to her at the time Stephen was born. You remember, Len, don't you? She said that she put a bowl of green dye on top of a mousetrap on a shelf in the larder and it went off, and the bowl turned upside down over her head, and her hair and face and her shoulders were green and stayed so for some days. It was Anna's home-made dye, and that was fast, if anything was."

The triplets giggled, though Margot, it must be confessed, less wholeheartedly than the other two.

"I don't think," Eve Hurrell said, "that dyes for cooking are likely to be quite so fierce as dyes for dyeing clothes. I've heard of that performance of Auntie Joey's. I heard about it from Mary-Lou Trelawney. She said none of you saw Auntie Joey for days."

"Yes. Well, suppose we get on with the job," Con said. "Margot, you had better go and put your head under the tap. Here's Len. She can come and see that you get thoroughly rinsed out. In the meantime, we had better get on with these sweets. Ruey, I think it would be an idea if you started to weigh out. We've got the bags over there. Weigh them out in grammes and half grammes and hand them on to those Fiveites who are doing nothing but stick around. They can tie up the bags and hand them on to their fellow members to pile them up in that big carton. And surely nobody can get into trouble doing that sort of thing!"

Unfortunately, once things start happening they are apt to go on, and this day's affair was no contradiction of that statement. Wanda von Eschenau, Jack Lambert, Margaret Twist and Samantha van der Byl had been put to shaking toffees up in a box of icing sugar before weighing them out. All had gone well at first, until Val Pertwee and Althea Glenyon came carrying a tray full of toffees contributed by other members of IVb to add to the general stock, and never noticed that Jocelyn Marvell was heading in the opposite direction with a wire tray piled high with coconut ice. They met head on and the resulting mess was something to be seen to be believed.

Icing sugar rose in clouds and in the middle of it all Robina McQueen was to be seen licking her fists to clear them of the sugar.

The next thing to occur was the upsetting of a tray full of pastilles, which Va had been weighing out into half gramme heaps ready for packing, but on this occasion no girl was to blame. Minette, who had been strolling about the lawn outside, suddenly glued her eyes to a large black Tom who called on her at intervals and was always repulsed with the most unladylike language. Seeing him now on HER lawn she swelled up, using unprintable language and made a dive for him. He was a bold fighter among his own sex, but little silvery Minette kept him well under a firm paw when he dared to venture near her. At sight of the spitting demon in front of the open french window he shot off, diving between the legs of the pastille bearer, who gave a squawk and parted with her tray in one direction, herself in another, while M. Noir produced a squawk on his own account and sought refuge in a nearby bush.

"It's a good thing," said Margot grimly as she and Ted Grantley directed a bevy from Inter V in picking up all they possibly could of the pastilles, "that what the eye doesn't see the heart doesn't grieve over. I think we *won't* report this! There you are, Jane, there's the last. For goodness sake take them away and get them bagged. And you go with her, Solange, and get it done as quickly as you can."

The pair retired in a state of wild giggles. Margot turned to see what was the next thing to do and uttered a hair-raising yell. Bruno, the Maynard family dog, had broken away from his mistress to come tearing across the two lawns to hurl himself on the first member of his own family which he saw—Margot. It is not easy to stand up under the weight of several pounds of excited St Bernard and Margot went flat. Bruno delightedly licked her face, then suddenly spying a couple of pastilles left on the ground he made away with them with one swipe of his tongue. It was at that point that Miss Annersley arrived with Len and some of the staff to see what was going on.

"Get up, Margot!" she exclaimed. "And who let that dog in here?"

"No one. He just came," Eve said.

"I might have known it. You're a bad boy, Bruno." She glanced round. "Ruey, take Bruno back home, please, and ask Mrs Maynard to keep him to quarters for the moment."

Ruey gave an involuntary grin and grabbed at Bruno's harness. "Come on, Bruno, you're a bad lad. You come home and we'll give your missus instructions." She went off with an unrepentant Bruno trotting beside her.

Miss Annersley turned to look at the piled up bags of confectionery on one large table. "What is this heap?" she inquired.

"That is what came from St Hilda's," Zoe Younge said. "They brought it early this morning before Frühstück. It's all priced ready."

"Good," Miss Annersley said briskly. "Then you had better pack it all together. I suppose it is the usual toffee and so on, so that will be ready to set out. Now what else have we got to consider before I go to the cakes?"

There was not a great deal left to do on the sweets now. The Head commented most favourably on the collection and then left them to pack the things in readiness for filling the stalls next day, while she and Len and half a dozen of the mistresses moved on to the big kitchens where the girls were busy with pastries and fancy cakes. Mdlle de Lachennais, Miss Ferrars, Miss Derwent, Miss Wilmot and Matron Henschell were hard at work filling pastries with jam.

Miss Carey, the handcrafts mistress, came in and looked round. "I want three people to come to handcrafts to collect the bon-bon baskets and carry them out here to be filled. Half a dozen other people will be needed for tying them. Who are the best at tying bows?"

At least a dozen people called out various names. She made her selection and they set to work. In the meantime Matey had departed to the school linen room where she sorted out sundry large damask tablecloths so that they could be taken down to

142

Hall ready for the girls to spread them early the next day on the trestle tables which did duty for stalls.

"Well," the Head observed when she had finished inspecting everything. "I think the Cakes and Sweets Stalls should do well. This afternoon you must rehearse the choruses for the concert and this evening most of you will be going for a ramble. By that time you will be tired of working on the Sale, and I am hoping that to-morrow will be cooler."

She mopped her face as she spoke. "In the meantime I think a glass of iced lemonade all round would be a good idea. Prefects, will you please see to it?" Which the prefects did con amore.

Chapter XII

NOISES IN THE NIGHT

THURSDAY morning broke fine and sunny, but there was a cool breeze coming from the North West which was greeted joyfully by everybody. At Frühstück Miss Annersley made an announcement which delighted everyone.

"You may speak your own language today; we will have Prayers at nine hours and after that the Juniors, Junior Middles and Kindergarten will go to the woods in charge of their own mistresses and some of the prefects. Senior Middles and Inter V will go up to the Röslein Alpe and gather branches to help deck the stalls. V a and b will go down towards Lauterbach and gather bracken to bring back for other decorations. The remaining prefects and VI Form will please go through the school and make sure that it is completely tidy. Those of you going out of the school will take your knapsacks with you and when you return you will go straight to your dormitories and lie down for an hour. Now do you understand that, everybody?"

Carmela looked up. "What about rehearsals?" she asked.

"You will have those after your rest. And now, thank you, Miss Lawrence." Miss Annersley nodded to Miss Lawrence, who was at the piano and who instantly struck into a gay march, and the girls marched out to their formrooms looking forward to a delightful day. They went upstairs to attend to dormitory duties and that done, went down again to the Splasheries to change into sandals and collect their knapsacks before marching along to the kitchen quarters where neat packages awaited them, together with flasks which contained, as they discovered later, iced fruit juice.

"Now," said Rosalie Dene, "we may hope for a little peace to get on with our various jobs. Will everyone here please read, mark, learn and inwardly digest the fact that I want all reports ready to copy into the Report Book by the end of this week." She looked severely at one or two ladies who were notorious for being late in this way.

"You and your old reports!" Nancy Wilmot grinned. "I think *you* have something to say, haven't you, Kathy?" She glanced at Miss Ferrars.

Kathy Ferrars nodded. "I want all geography books handed in, duly signed off by the form mistress, *also* by Saturday. I think that's all I do want, though."

Peace reigned over the school the whole of the first half of the morning. It was broken by a series of shrieks from the kitchen quarters. Matey, speeding down the stairs and along the corridor leading to the kitchens, dashed in to find three of the maids standing petrified looking at a tiny snake which had somehow found its way in. Snakes are not very numerous in the Oberland and most of those found are harmless enough, but this particular one was a viper. It was later discovered that it had been brought in in a basket of vegetables and the terrified maids knew just enough to know that it was venomous and angry.

Matey never hesitated. She snatched up a large pan and brought it heavily down on the hissing reptile at the exact moment that Gaudenz entered the kitchens. He was a big man but he was quick in the uptake. Before the raging creature could recover from the shrewd blow Matey had administered he was standing on its head and literally fulfilling the Scriptural command, crushing the thing with all his weight.

Matey, like Gaudenz, acted at once. She pushed the terrified girls into the arms of Cook Karen and left her to deal with them, while she herself summoned another of the men to come and tackle what was left of the snake.

"Where did it come from?" Matey demanded when the intruder had received its quietus and been carried off to the incinerator by one of the boys. Gaudenz rumbled deeply in his chest.

"It must have come with the spinach from Frau Unseli," Karen said firmly. "She told me that they had discovered a nest under the bank in the vegetable patch but she thought they had killed all the little ones. This must be one that has escaped." She fixed a firm eye on one of the sobbing girls and continued, "Cease thy noise, foolish one! The snake is dead, it has not bitten thee. Wherefore all this brou-ha-ha? Go down to the cellars and sort the potatoes for the potato salad to-night. Go with her, Mechtilde, and bring enough. Go!"

They fled. Karen was very much mistress of her own domain. She was good to the girls but she had them at a word. Matey turned to Gaudenz. "Better go through all those vegetables," she said briskly. "We do not want a repetition of this. Neither do we desire to have the Unseli vipers, so just make sure, will you?" He nodded and went off and Matey retired to the Head's study to report on the latest alarm.

"Good heavens!" exclaimed Miss Annersley. "You're quite right, Matey. We don't want any other snakes than we have of our own. This Platz is remarkably free from pests of that kind; even in the woods we don't get many, and I'll be glad if we can keep clear. The girls were all right, weren't they?"

"Oh scared!" Matey said. "You would expect that. But the thing was killed before it could do any harm."

"I hope," said Miss Annersley thoughtfully, "that we are not going to start trouble of that kind up here. It happened once some years ago; actually in Tirol. There seemed to be a positive plague of vipers and there were one or two rather nasty accidents with visitors. I've never known another. We must just warn everybody to keep a look-out. And luckily term is very nearly at an end." Then she turned her attention to the list of curtains required for

146

the new dormitories that were coming into being next term. This was not a very easy matter to decide, for there were so many dormitories already to take the names of the different flowers that finding new names was something of a puzzle.

Rehearsals were now in full swing for choruses, country dances and the various one-act plays which were being produced by the elder girls. The bell rang for Break and the people who had been kept behind for one reason or another swarmed into the Speisesaal to see how Karen had treated them with regard to drinks and biscuits. She had made no difference. They had fruit drinks and three biscuits each.

"And that," said Lesley Anderson disgustedly, "is not what I should have expected of Karen on such a day as this. She might have spread herself a little."

The early afternoon brought back the lower part of the school for its rest and then for a rehearsal with the orchestra in the choruses belonging to the sundry cantatas—three, to be exact—which were to provide entertainments on THE DAY.

By this time Gaudenz and Co had got the stalls erected and the Maypole with its varied ribbons set up on one of the front lawns, and now he was directing his followers in the making of a Welcome Arch over the gates. It was at this point that the telephone pealed loudly from the office. Rosalie Dene dropped the boxes of drawing pins she had come to collect on her desk and took up the receiver. As she did so she murmured to herself, "Now I wonder just what horrid shock is in store for us!"

She knew almost at once. Lady Carew, mother of Jane Carew of Vb and a well-known Shakespearean actress, had agreed to come and open the Sale. This telephone message was to say that she had slipped on the stairs of her hotel and fallen full length. Luckily no serious damage had been done but she had wrenched an ankle very badly and would certainly not be fit for the next few days for any ceremony such as opening a Sale. The horrified

Rosalie took the message and then went to seek the Head. Miss Annersley was not easily to be found. At last she turned up in Matey's room where she was having a splinter removed from her finger.

"Do you want me?" she inquired.

"*Will* you stand still," Matey demanded in irritated tones. "Ah, there it is! That's got him! Now soak it in that bowl. Right! Now let me see—oh, a little bit of sticking plaster, I think."

The Head smiled and looked at Rosalie. What she saw in that young woman's face wiped the smile off her own. "Oh, *what* now?" she asked.

"The crowning blow," Rosalie said, not mincing matters. "Lady Carew has had a fall on the stairs, wrenched her ankle badly and won't be able to come on Saturday."

"What? But this is Thursday afternoon!" Miss Annersley gasped. "How are we to find anyone to take over in the time?"

"We must," said Rosalie firmly. "Madge is no use, of course. She's coming over to-morrow, but they're breaking the journey somewhere because of an appointment for Jem on Friday, so they are staying in Geneva overnight and coming on early Saturday morning. We can't ask her to open the Sale."

Miss Annersley's face lit up. "But of course we can," she exclaimed. "You get on to their hotel and leave a message for her to ring up as soon as they get there. Then I'll have a word with her."

"And what will you do if she won't or can't do it?" Rosalie asked.

"Ask Joey, of course," Miss Annersley said crisply. "Now that's settled."

Rosalie chuckled. "Knowing Joey, yes. But she'll have plenty to say before she agrees."

It came as quite a shock when Joey, approached on the subject when she appeared in the school garden later that afternoon, said amiably, "With all the pleasure in life, my dear. And, by the way, have you heard anything from Tom Gay, or isn't she providing us with a house this year?"

"I had a letter from her this morning," Miss Annersley replied. "And the usual should be arriving to-morrow."

"I thought you were taking it rather calmly," Joey remarked. "Now will that be all we have to think about, Hilda? What with one thing and another I never knew a Sale require so much preparation."

"Only arranging the things on the various stalls, and putting out small tables and chairs in one of the sunk gardens for use as a café. And both those are the girls' concern. Gaudenz and his helpers will bring out the necessary forms and chairs for people to sit on during the concerts, etc, but they'll do that early on Saturday morning as usual."

By this time the mistresses, having finished their sundry tasks, had begun to assemble. They sighed thankfully as they sank down into garden chairs. The day had certainly been cooler but they had been working to their limit and they were glad of a short reprieve.

Big Nancy Wilmot mopped her brow freely and heaved a vast sigh. "I don't know about the rest of you," she said feelingly, "but I for one could do with a long cold drink."

"There's plenty in the Speisesaal," little Miss Andrews said. "The maids were bringing in jugs of Karen's famous fruit drink when I came through ten minutes ago, and there are beakers on the shelves."

"Be a gem and fetch some," Miss Derwent said. "I've still got two lots of reports to finish before I go to my bed to-night. Then that does finish it for me, thank goodness."

"If you please, Miss Dene, you're wanted on the phone." This was Jocelyn at her most proper.

"Thank you, Jocelyn." Rosalie Dene got to her feet with a

sigh of resignation. "Don't drink all the fruit juice. Leave some for me," she said, addressing the party at large. Then she went off followed by Jocelyn.

The gong sounded for Abendessen which was followed by Prayers once the tables had been cleared, and thereafter bed for the Juniors while the Middles and Seniors took their leisure in the gardens until their turn came. It must be owned that the staff were only too glad to follow their pupils' example and retire to bed at a comparatively early hour, and silence, broken only by the sounds of a summer evening, fell over the shelf.

It was going on for midnight when Jack Lambert woke up suddenly with an uneasy feeling that all was not well. She was dormitory prefect and her first idea was that somebody was breaking dormitory rules.

"I'll show them, whoever it is," she thought vengefully, as she pulled on her dressing-gown and wriggled her feet into her bedroom slippers.

She pulled the cubicle curtains aside, slipped out and stood looking through the moonlit room up and down the dormitory. So far as she could see all was well. But Jack had not been all these years at school for nothing. She listened. No, there was no half-smothered giggling, so whatever was happening rule-breaking seemed to have nothing to do with it. The next thing was to tiptoe from cubicle to cubicle, part the curtains cautiously and peer in. All was well.

"And yet," Jack said to herself, "I'll swear there's something up. The thing is, what? Could it be one of the other dormitories?"

With Jack to think was to act. She cautiously turned the handle of the dormitory door and slid out into the corridor through the narrowest slit possible. Again all was quiet. Could it be something downstairs, she wondered? She went to the bannisters to hang over. She could hear nothing nor could she see anything.

By this time Jack was fully intrigued. Could it be burglars? In that case what were they after? "I think," she said to herself, "this is where I'm going to need help. Now let me think! Wanda—no use. Val Gardiner—yes! And I'd better go to Crocus and collect Jane, Copper and Judy Willoughby. Now! Jane and Copper can sneak upstairs and take one each end of the upstairs corridor. I'll send Val and Judy on to the top floor. Then I'll call Ailie Russell, as she's close at hand, to be my partner. No need to disturb Matey. We will be quiet enough for any burglar."

She proceeded to carry out her schemes. She had to combat some excitement from Val Gardiner, who was always easily excited, not to speak of Ailie Russell, who wanted to know who or what it was.

"If we wait long enough we'll find out no doubt," Jack snapped at her in the lowest tone possible. "Come out into the corridor. Val's out there, and the two of you can hang on while I go to Crocus and get some more people."

How she contrived to get her party together without rousing the entire corridor was something neither she nor anyone else could ever explain. She did it in the end and then detailed her plan to the others, slipping from one sentinel to another, keeping them all thoroughly on the qui vive and listening hard all the time for any alien sounds she might catch.

Meanwhile people in some of the other houses of the School were being disturbed. Len Maynard sat up in bed and listened; decided that the vague sounds—alien sounds—she could hear came from outside; pulled on her jeans and a sweater which she had left ready for a final weeding early in the morning and went out into the corridor. The sounds were growing louder, distant rough voices mingled with a thudding of feet, coming nearer as she listened. Doors in the corridor were opening and more prefects were coming out, roused as Len had been. The noise outside increased. Furious shouts, sudden yells and the sound of feet were growing louder every minute. Len turned quickly to Ted Grantley who had just emerged from her dormitory.

"Ted, I'm going to the Annexe to rouse the Head if she isn't roused already. You go and stand by the alarm bell ready to ring it the instant you're told. I don't know what's happening but it sounds like a revolution."

Ted shot off while Len, putting all ceremony aside, made for the Annexe, swung open the baize door which shut it off from the rest of the School and raced up the stairs to the bedrooms, to be met at the head of the stairs by a calm Miss Annersley who said, "Ah, Len! I don't know what's happening, but Miss Dene is ringing up the police. In the meantime I want everyone to get into gardening kit and then go quietly downstairs to Hall and wait there till someone comes to tell you what to do. Please take charge."

"What about ringing the alarm bell?"

"I doubt if there is any need. Listen!" as the stillness of the night was rent by long-drawn yells.

"What about Mamma?" Len asked.

"Your father is at home to-night and will see to her and the little ones."

"Yes," Len said. "What do you think it is?"

"A set of uncontrolled young fools like those who are creating disturbances all over just now. Go and attend to your duties, Len." And Len went.

Meanwhile the noise of battle was growing steadily louder. The school saw to it that the girls were safely gathered together, prefects and mistresses took firm charge, but all of them, listening to the increasing tumult outside, realized that a very nasty situation seemed to be building up.

"What's it all in aid of?" Althea demanded of Jocelyn as they met on the corridor.

"No talking on the corridor," said the stern voice of Margot

Maynard. "Who was that? You, Althea? Be quiet. All of you be quiet," and in an aside to Eve she muttered, "There's row enough going on without *them* starting."

It was thanks to this sort of thing from the prefects that there was no panic among the girls. They were marched down to Hall where, once the mistresses had taken the roll they were told to sit on the floor and wait for further orders.

In the meantime, judging from the sounds drifting up from further down the mountain a free-for-all fight was in full swing. What really *was* alarming was the sound of one or two pistol shots.

"Quite a nasty, sticky situation," observed an unexpected voice behind Miss Annersley as that lady came into her own little salon. She turned with a gasp.

"Mary-Lou!" she exclaimed. "What on earth are you doing here?"

Mary-Lou Trelawney, once Head Girl and now, like Mrs Maynard, almost a legend in the school, beamed down on her from her height of five foot eight.

"Well," she said, "if you really want to know, I came up with the troops."

"What?"

"Well, about a dozen of the Polizei."

"Oh, so they have started them off," the Head said. "Good! I haven't heard yet what is the why of all this. Do you know anything, Mary-Lou?"

"Well, I've heard three or four stories," Mary-Lou said, collapsing into a chair. "One is that it's a bunch of undergraduates making nuisances of themselves as usual. Another is that it's a gang after some millionaire or other who's up in this direction. Either may be correct."

"I'm afraid it's the second," the Head said grimly. "The Bachofen girl is up here at the San; her people are staying in one of the guest houses. He is the big millionaire ship-builder from Denmark, and they've been afraid for some time of kidnappers. They have a bodyguard, of course, but if there's a gang out in force that's not much help."

"What's wrong with the girl?" Mary-Lou asked.

"Last stages of T.B., though her parents won't believe it, and what she knows I haven't the least idea."

Mary-Lou's merry face grew grave. "That's rather awful. Surely even gangsters would draw the line at kidnapping a dying girl."

"Apparently not." Miss Annersley spoke with great bitterness. "The longer I live, Mary-Lou, the more horrified I am at the growing wickedness of the world. Well, what are you doing here, anyhow?" She changed the subject.

"I came up for the Sale, of course. Little did I think I was going to be landed in this sort of affair." She got no further. There was a sharp rap at the door, which opened to show an officer of the Polizei, who saluted.

"Madame, I am here to announce that all is well. We have taken the ringleaders and half a dozen others and be assured that those who have escaped will be met and captured further down. It is all over. We will leave guards on the paths for the next day or two, but you may stay calm. All will be well."

"And," said Miss Annersley as he finally left amid a hurricane of compliments, "I hope that he is right. I have had all the excitement I want for one term. In fact, for the remainder of the year. And now, Mary-Lou, where are you proposing to put up?"

"At Freudesheim, I shouldn't like to face Joey if I didn't. I think I had better be getting along there, just to show myself. I'll come back later," she added encouragingly, "and help with anything you want."

"Thank you," Miss Annersley said. "I'm sure you'll be a great help. I won't ask for your own news just now. I'll hear that when the Sale is over."

Mary-Lou betook herself to Freudesheim. Miss Annersley turned to Rosalie Dene, who came up at that moment.

"There's one blessing. The girls can sleep late without interfering with the time-table. Get them off to bed as fast as you can. The rising bell can sound two hours later than usual. And that will even matters up considerably." She looked at Rosalie. "Send everyone off, Rosalie. Ask the staff to make sure everyone gets to bed as quickly as possible."

Rosalie nodded. "It's the best thing we can do, and we can pack them all off early to-morrow night, or to-night now, I suppose. And you, my dear," she added, "can set us all the example and depart yourself. Matey—where's Matey? You might see that Hilda goes to bed at once or she'll be dead by the time the Sale starts."

"You don't have to tell me," said Matey who had just arrived. She fixed the Head with a glare. "Off you go!"

Miss Annersley might be the Head of the Chalet School but when Matey spoke in a certain tone she submitted to orders as meekly as any of the girls. In fact, as Jo said, they all did.

Nothing more happened before Mittagessen. Mary-Lou arrived at nine o'clock all prepared for the fray. "What would you like me to do?" she inquired affably of Miss Annersley, meeting that lady in the entrance hall on her way to the Speisesaal for Frühstück.

"Have you had breakfast?" the Head asked. Mary-Lou nodded.

"Joey's family are early birds and as they slept through all that disturbance last night breakfast was at the usual time. But I can always drink an extra cup of coffee. I'll come in and have one with you and we'll discuss what my job for the morning is to be."

"I think we had better leave you a free-lance to help out where and when required. Now come along to the Speisesaal." She led the way as the gong sounded and it was evidence of the fact that this was no ordinary school day that the girls broke into a chorus of exclamations of "Mary-Lou! Oh Hurrah!"

"Grace," said the Head in a quiet tone. "You may welcome Mary-Lou later."

Mary-Lou went crimson, dropped her long lashes over her eyes and looked foolish. She had not expected such very public recognition. Joey told her later that she might have expected it if she had even given it a thought.

"Well, I didn't," Mary-Lou said crossly. "Silly little goops! And all of them staring at me as if I was the ninth wonder of the world!"

"Oh, I know," Joey said. "I've been through it myself." Then she suggested that Mary-Lou should help to wheel the trolley loaded with small dishes of fruit to the head of the centre sunk garden where various members of Va were waiting for it, and thereafter they were kept so busy they had no time for idle gossip.

Nothing more untoward happened during the morning. The tables were finally made ready to receive the goods and great sheets of brown paper were cut up to various sizes and shapes to cover some of the oddly shaped things that would bedeck the stalls.

The prefects, meeting at the gate into the playing fields some ten minutes or so before the gong sounded for Mittagessen, looked across the busy scene.

"Ay di me!" sighed Louise Grunbaum, "this is the last time I shall do this. *We* shall do this, for that applies to all of us."

Ted Grantley grinned at her. "Like the walrus, I shed a bitter tear. Come off it, Louise! You never know what might happen, and in any case, this is not the time to be morbid."

"Ah, but you English, you have no sentiment," sighed Louise.

"No sentimentality, you mean," Margot said brusquely. "You Germans are *all* sentimentality."

"Shall we herd those young monkeys into line?" Audrey Everett demanded.

"We must. There goes the gong," Primrose Trevoase rejoined. It was certainly not easy to get the Junior members of the school into their usual trim lines. They were all far too excited for that; and various members of Inter V nearly got themselves turned out to the punishment table which, as Jack Lambert, the Form Prefect, pointed out with much firmness, would have been an unheard of disgrace.

"And if it comes off, what do you think the Head would have to say?" Jack wound up. "Probably turn us all out of the Sale and a nice thing that would be!" Since according to their way of thinking nothing was more likely this awful suggestion sobered them down and nobody had any reason to complain of their behaviour for the next hour or so.

The next thing was the bringing of the trolleys, heavily laden, to the various stands and stalls. They were stripped of their loads, which were placed under the stalls for the moment, and the trolleys were wheeled back for further loads when there came an imperative cry "Clear the decks!"

No need to ask what that meant. Tom Gay's annual offering had arrived. "I'm just *thrilled* to know what form it takes this year," Peggy Burnett confided to her colleague Kathy Ferrars. "Tom has rung the changes so often I don't see how she can manage it this time."

Kathy laughed. "It wouldn't surprise me in the least if she's gone full length, though I don't quite see how she can have done."

Matey, standing near, overheard. "She's always managed it so far, though whether she does it herself or gets advice from other people I have yet to know. But, like you, Kathy, I should be surprised at nothing. After all, I've known Tom for a good many years."

By this time the men were wheeling an enormous case towards the big trestle table which had been set aside to take Tom's model, whatever it might be. Slowly, carefully, the packing case was lifted on to the table, and an envelope was handed to the Head, who had come to receive it. She opened it with some curiosity.

"Good gracious," she exclaimed, as she glanced at its contents. "This is merely instructions as to what to do with the packing case. Ah, there you are, Gaudenz. Miss Gay says that we are to unscrew the four end panels, the case will then drop apart and can be removed. She asks us to preserve the panels and let her have them back sometime. Also the screws."

"Is she coming herself this time?" queried Nancy Wilmot.

"That's absolutely all she says—instructions about opening the case. You'd better go ahead, Gaudenz." The Head turned to the big man who was standing by grinning and Gaudenz set to work to unscrew the panels. He was very careful to preserve the screws in a special pocket in his working coat and he piled the panels one on top of the other as they fell apart. The last one dropped and revealed to their gaze a series of small boxes which were taken away and piled up at one side, when at last their curiosity was rewarded and they were gazing at the model of an old country inn, complete with dangling sign—carefully covered over—and with a courtyard, stabling and all the other etceteras.

Mary-Lou, who had gone back to Joey's for Mittagessen, arrived back at the school just as the Inn was uncovered and her first comment was "What's the name of the place? Why has Tom covered the sign over?"

"I was wondering that myself. We shall probably find some sort of explanation when we've got the whole thing unpacked."

Everyone looking at the Inn was delighted and a chorus of admiration rose, but there was more to come. When the boxes were opened, they were found to contain old-fashioned settles, tables, a hay-ladder to fasten to the loft door at one end, and all the other appurtenances of a really old-fashioned English inn, including model horses for the stables, a coach, a beautifully made little post chaise and dolls dressed as ostler, landlord and even a jolly barman.

Other boxes held tiny glasses, tankards—"and where Tom got hold of those, goodness only knows," Ruth Derwent murmured to Nancy Wilmot. It really was an outstanding effort. Finally out of the largest cask came a much folded-up note.

"I thought I was done in this time, but this was finally suggested to me. I hope you like it. Please admire the tankards. They were made by one of my boys who wants to go in for that sort of thing; not tankards but trinkets. I think he has managed marvellously. The glass things came from a firm of glass blowers who visited our shop and were very much taken with what they saw of the Inn as it then was, and offered to send a set of glasses. In fact, the old boy was all over it. So much so that he ordered a facsimile as an advertisement for their firm. So that has done the Club quite a lot of good, and what is more, has done one or two of our lads even more good, because it has brought their work so much more before the public. Now for the competition.

"I am sorry to say I have had to fall back on a very old competition but really there didn't seem to be anything else which would fit the bill, but it *has* got a twist in it. How many of you have noticed that the Inn sign is covered up? There's a purpose in that. Because this competition consists in guessing the name of the Inn. I'll give you one clue. There is a reference to an animal. Now that's all the help you're getting from me. So good luck to you all and may the best man win."

Just as Miss Annersley finished reading this aloud there was an exclamation behind her and she swung round, startled.

"Madge Russell!" she exclaimed. "When did you come?"

"Oh, just now," said Lady Russell nonchalantly. "Never mind me. Tell me, is this Tom's latest? Well, I think she's excelled herself. Look at the darling little stalls for horses. Oh, and those settles are too delightful for words."

"See the beer barrels and the bottles of wine!" Peggy Burnett pointed them out.

"What I like," said Nancy Wilmot, "is the kennel with the noble hound. Look at him! You can see he's just going to give tongue."

"Yes," said Miss Annersley briskly, "and if you crowd had your own way you'd spend the rest of the afternoon exclaiming. However, we've got to put up the screens round it and secure the tarpaulins over them so that no one else can see it until it's ready."

Feeling and looking rather conscience-stricken, the younger mistresses set to work with a will, while the Head and Lady Russell moved a little to one side for a few words of greeting.

"Are you staying here?" Miss Annersley said.

"Give me a chance," her friend retorted. "Do you want me to be murdered?"

"Not particularly. It would cast a gloom over the later proceedings if you were. But who is going to be so violent?"

"Hilda Annersley, have you suddenly gone dumb? Where would Jo be?"

"Dear me. I'd forgotten about Jo," said the Head. She gave a sudden grin. "What a shock she'd get if she heard me! Well, go on and give us the hanes."

"Well, Jem had to come with a patient, so I came with them; flying, of course. And I meant to let you know, but what with one thing and another I didn't manage it. For one thing the twins' school has had to go into quarantine the week before they break up for the summer holidays and with scarlet fever, of all things, if you please!"

"Oh, Madge, no!" Miss Annersley exclaimed.

"Unfortunately it's yes," Lady Russell said. "It simply finishes their holidays. Just what the school is going to do I don't know yet, but anyhow it put everything else out of my mind or very nearly so. I did manage to remember the School Sale. Who have you got to open it?"

With one voice each of the staff who had overheard this exclaimed, "YOU!"

"What? Me? But you can't! You've given me no warning. I haven't a thing ready. I haven't even a frock with me that would suit a lady opener."

"Don't worry," said Nancy Wilmot. "We'll all rally round as far as clothes are concerned. And you know perfectly well that you're never at a loss for words. So that's that!"

And protest she never so much, that, as far as the horrified Lady Russell was concerned, remained that.

Chapter XIII

THE SALE

THE Sale opened with a march past of the Seasons, each headed by its own special prefect. The floating robes of the Four Seasons made an excellent beginning to the parade. They were followed by various flowers at the moment very fresh and dainty in crepe paper. What it would be like by the end of the Sale was, to quote Ted, "anyone's guess". They marched past the staff, and then the characters applicable to the various Seasons took their turn. As they reached their stalls, each took up position and last instructions were hastily given, for already the visitors were reaching the gates, where John Peel and sundry other well-known characters waited to sell tickets of admission.

"It looks," observed Con before she slipped away to the bookstall, "as though we are going to be packed out. Come along, people, do your duty!"

"Oh, Con, but how can we, when the Sale is not yet open?" Carmela asked, "and who is going to open it?"

"Didn't you listen at Prayers?" Con demanded. "The Head said that Lady Russell had arrived unexpectedly and *she* would open it."

"Ah, see, they come!" cried Carmela, pointing dramatically to the main building, from the great doors of which came a stately procession headed by Miss Annersley with Lady Russell, Joey with Miss Wilson, the Head of St Mildred's, the finishing branch of the Chalet School, several of the doctors from the Sanatorium, likewise the Matron. The company paraded down the broad drive, when something quite unrehearsed and certainly not desired, took place. Bruno had been chained up for the morning but somehow he had worked the chain loose and now he solemnly put himself at the head of the entire crowd, reducing his mistress to fits of smothered giggles and making Ted and Len clutch each other in dismay. Visitors, meanwhile, were pouring in by the lower path and were being ushered to their places by bunches of girls, who were far too busy to pay much attention to Bruno. So the gentleman led the way up to the table behind which the Lady Opener, together with the two Heads and half a dozen other important people were to take their places. They took their places and Bruno spread himself full length in front of them.

"Joey!" hissed Miss Annersley in an agitated whisper. "Get that dog away."

Joey grinned. "Easier said than done, my dear. Leave him alone. He'll be good."

She was quite right. Bruno behaved like a gentleman throughout the whole proceedings, but he stayed where he was, looking very pleased with himself. Miss Annersley glared at Jo but said no more, while Miss Wilson, who had a strong sense of humour, had to suppress a strong desire to laugh as she saw Joey's complacent expression.

Miss Wilson and Miss Annersley had originally been Co-Heads of the Chalet School, but when St Mildred's was started, Miss Wilson had gone there as Head, while Miss Annersley remained as Head of the Chalet School proper. They had always been great friends and they often spent evenings together in their free time. Needless to say, Miss Wilson, together with her pupils, never missed attending the annual Sale.

Lady Russell knew exactly what was required of her. She welcomed the visitors, explained the aims of the Sale as concisely as she could and then declared it open. Dr Maynard proposed a vote of thanks, which was seconded by one of the younger doctors and carried unanimously. And then, led by Lady Russell, the visitors scattered all over the grounds to inspect the stalls and their contents.

Mary-Lou had come with Joey to the Sale. Not being one of the V.I.P.s she parted with that lady, giving vent to a sudden exclamation of delight. Joey was unable to see why she seemed so pleased and was nearly frantic with curiosity, but was obliged to go to take her place in the procession while Mary-Lou grabbed the hands of a jolly looking young woman of her own age with a smothered exclamation of "Vi Lucy! I didn't know you were coming."

"Well, come to that, I didn't know *you* were coming," retorted her friend. "I thought Hilda Jukes might be here, because she's somewhere in the neighbourhood, but one never knows where you are."

"You sound as if I were a gypsy," said Mary-Lou indignantly. Her blue eyes rested on the charming face smiling at her. "Lovely as ever. You always were one of the School's beauties."

"Well, there's a nice thing to say!" Viola Lucy sounded quite as indignant as her friend. "If that's all you can remember me for I don't think much of it."

Mary-Lou chuckled. "Oh, I *have* a few other memories. But how gorgeous meeting you! Let's go and bag seats somewhere where we can have a good old natter. Oh, by the way, how do you like my new kit?"

Vi regarded her dainty green frock and shady black hat. "I like it," she said with decision. "And now just return the compliment. How do you like *my* kit?"

Mary-Lou grinned broadly. "You know perfectly well that you were born knowing how to dress. I had to learn, and a great bore it's been."

"Still, you have learnt it," Vi pointed out. "Come on, let's see who we can collect, and we'll get all the hanes."

Later, during Dr Maynard's vote of thanks to Lady Russell,

Mary-Lou suddenly grabbed Vi's arm. "Vi! Bruno!"

"What about Bruno?" Vi asked startled.

"Let's give him a collecting box and I'll take him round."

"That's an idea," Vi said cordially, "but you want two collecting boxes, one attached to each side of his harness. You take him on for the first hour, then I'll relieve you for another one."

"Excellent scheme. After all, why shouldn't Bruno do his share?" She clapped the sides of the big amber-coated gentleman who had left his post on recognizing Mary-Lou and Vi and padded solemnly across to them, his great tail swinging delightedly, to Joey's amusement and Miss Annersley's horror. However, all was well, for Vi and Mary-Lou took the gentleman off with them and when next the apprehensive Head saw him, he was strolling among the crowds with Mary-Lou and making it quite plain that he expected people to put something in his collecting boxes, which the bright pair had duly affixed to his harness.

By this time a number of people were gathered round the model of the Inn. A table with forms on either side had been set up and people wishing to enter for the competition were given slips of paper and pencils to inscribe their guesses and their names and addresses, and were requested to pay five francs for each entry to the members of Va who were in charge of the whole affair.

There were other competitions, of course, also a number of draws. The Domestic Science people had produced six elaborate cakes; Mdlle's needlework classes were responsible for exquisitely sewn nightdresses and other garments whose delicate embroidery set their value at much more than ordinary bazaar prices, and one beautifully-worked broderie anglaise tablecloth given by Mdlle herself was discovered at the end of the Sale to have brought in two hundred and fifty francs.

In the Winter section were books, jigsaws, bric-à-brac and all the little things that would come in useful for Christmas presents.

One huge fir had been turned into a Christmas Tree and with Christmas fairies skipping round and attending to the purchasers it gave a most inviting effect.

Autumn was distinguished by Matey's usual contribution of jam and bottled fruits, to say nothing of the Domestic Science's supreme effort, a beautifully cooked and handsomely adorned Boar's Head.

Spring's special effort was to be found on the china stall. Everyone who could had contributed at least one article to this, and the variety, together with the lovely colouring of much of the pottery and china, made a glow of colour.

Summer was responsible for the refreshments and therefore was in charge of the sunk gardens. The Kindergarten people acted as messengers: in short, everybody was fully occupied for the whole of the morning.

About noon Dr Maynard put in a second appearance to take charge of the clock golf for a short time before handing it over to Reg Entwistle, who came along to do his share, while Jack Maynard himself was summoned to welcome the incoming ambulances at the Sanatorium. Len, hurrying past the office, glanced in and saw Reg as he parted from her father, whose instructions were, "Go and take hold of the clock golf for the next half-hour or so. I'll send someone to relieve you then."

Len paused to say, "Hullo! So you've come to help. Good!"

"Don't I always?" Reg demanded in injured tones.

"No, not always," Len returned firmly. "I've known occasions when you've simply slid out of it."

"Not for several years now," Reg said, giving her a meaning look.

Len went faintly pink. "Don't talk nonsense," she said sharply. "In any case I can't stop to talk at all. I must run," and she sped off.

Reg looked after her and sighed. "I wish she'd grow up," he

said to himself. "It's all very well being matey, but I want more than that. A heck of a lot more than that." However, it was no use wishing. He could only wait and, as far as possible, see to it that no one else took his place, and it wasn't going to be easy once Len had gone to Oxford.

Meanwhile Len had hurried on and found herself embroiled in an argument between half a dozen Senior Middles, headed by Erica Standish. They heaved themselves at Len.

"Len!" cried Erica. "Sunflowers belong to Summer, don't they?"

"No, they're Autumn," cried Emelie St Laurent, equally fiercely.

"I'm sorry, Emelie, but you're wrong," Len told her firmly. "They're summer flowers, come in August."

There was a moment's silence, then Erica rubbed it in with one of the most unwelcome remarks there is, "*Told* you so!"

"There's no need for that," Len informed Erica. "Emelie, would you mind going over to the bookstall and asking someone in charge there to look through my order and see how many books I've got?"

"Ah, oui, Len," Emelie exclaimed, and went off in a hurry.

Len looked down at Erica. "Do you *want* to start any trouble today?" she inquired suavely.

"Er—er—no!" Erica stammered. "Only Emelie was so maddening."

"So I expect were you," the Head Girl told her. "But in any case, Erica, there isn't time for private feuds today. Scrap, if scrap you must, to-morrow. And the rest of you," she added, "don't stand there doing nothing. Go and see what you can do to help. Scram!"

They vanished. As Samaris Davies had once remarked, Len was a pet, but what she said went. If you knew what was good for you, you did as she told you and no argument.

By this time the Sale was in full swing; the visitors were being pursued by the various folk in charge of the draws as well as being attended to by others in charge of the stalls. The dozen or so men who had so far turned up were being tactfully led to the clock golf, and the tinies who had come with visiting parents were being left in the nursery which was in charge of three of the Matrons headed by Matron Henschell, who from her earliest days had been a favourite with the younger ones, and three or four of the Sixth. This was a new effort for the Sale. It had been suggested by Ted Grantley, who pointed out how very much easier it would be for mothers if they could leave their infants in safe keeping. The Matrons would be able to cope with teething babies, if any; if necessary, bottles could be prepared and the tinies who needed long naps could be tucked away from all the noise of the Sale proper. A token payment would help to add considerably to the Sale funds, so that taking it all round the idea had been welcomed with acclamation.

Maria Zinkel had pointed out that they could add another division and take in the tinies up to the age of five and had offered to take charge there with some of her friends.

"This *is* a good idea," one young mother remarked to Nancy Wilmot, as she returned from handing her small daughter over to Maria. "You don't want tinies trotting after you all the time, they grow tired and cross, and it's difficult to leave them in a hotel. But this is a splendid effort, and now, Nancy, give me all the news while we drink a cup of coffee together." And the pair went off to one of the sunk gardens to enjoy some iced coffee and a good gossip.

The notices about the Sale which had been distributed to the various hotels in Interlaken and displayed in the town had stated that visitors wishing to spend the whole day at the Sale could obtain lunch at the various Gasthausen on the Platz, and towards lunch time the visitors from a distance began to drift off in search of a meal. They were firmly reminded by the members of the Sixth in charge of the gate that they must produce their admission tickets when they returned if they didn't want to pay a second time!

As for the School, they had been sent in relays to the Speisesaal for a meal consisting of iced salad, minced meat in aspic, followed by ices, and the whole washed down with the School's own special fruit drink. The Juniors had all been packed off to lie down on their beds for the usual rest hour; the others were far too busy for that today. Joey had rushed home to make sure that the twins were well; it seemed so short a time since they had been living on edge about little Phil that even now, when there was talk of Geoff and Phil joining the Kindergarten next term, she could scarcely believe it.

She had taken Bruno with her to have a token meal, promising Mary-Lou to bring him back with her when she returned. Mary-Lou herself with Vi had joined the school in their cold lunch, to the delight of the girls who remembered them.

"What's the first important thing?" Madge Russell asked the Head as they came out from Mittagessen which they had had in the Annexe with the other important guests.

"Well, that partly depends on you."

"Me?"

"Well, what do you want to see? Would you like to see the crowning of the May Queen, the Harvest Festival, the Christmas Party, or the Cantata?"

"On the whole," said Madge, "I think I should like to see the crowning of the May Queen. Where is it?"

"Right front lawn."

"Good. Lead me there."

Miss Annersley laughed. "You can take yourself there, my dear. It's a very good choice," she added as she left her guest to stare after her and wonder what she meant. She was soon to know. Joey arrived.

"Well, I suppose I'd better come with you," remarked the younger sister.

Madge stopped short. "Why?" she asked suspiciously.

"Well, I suppose I'd better see my own niece crowned."

"Are you telling me Ailie is the May Queen?" Madge demanded.

"Didn't you know? How very remiss of Ailie not to tell you. Yes, she's the May Queen. Come along and we'll bag seats. My own Felicity is also in that episode. She and three others are doing a dance. Now come along. I think—yes, those two seats. Are they booked, Melanie, or may we have them?"

"No seats are booked," Melanie said severely.

"I see. You pays your money and you takes your choice," Jo said enthusiastically. "Excellent scheme. Who do we pay?"

"Me, as I'm here," Melanie told her as they secured their seats.

Other people were following their example and the forms and chairs set round the lawn on three sides were filling up rapidly. Before long they were practically full and then there came the Old English Maypole Song, "Come to the Maypole, haste away, for it is now a holiday," and the Maypole dancers came skipping in, followed by Jack in the Green, the four knights of Britain—St George, St Andrew, St Patrick and St David—a team of sword dancers and several Morris teams.

"How long are you giving to this?" Madge inquired.

"I think it's an hour," Joey said, waving vehemently at a member of Lower IVb, who was carrying a tray piled with paper fans. "How much are your fans, Brigit?"

"Ten francs each," Brigit replied.

"I'll take a couple. Here you are. Thank you."

"Mrs Maynard, some of Inter V are selling Japanese umbrellas, if you'd like one of those."

"In that case we'll have to move to the back," Madge said. "Other people simply won't be able to see a thing. But considering what the sun is doing I think it wouldn't be a bad idea. You go and see if you can bag two seats while I collect one sunshade between us. Who has them, Brigit?"

"Well, Jack Lambert for one, Wanda von Eschenau for another, and Valerie Gardiner for a third."

"Well, send one of them over with a sunshade, will you? And tell her—Ah, Mrs Maynard has succeeded in getting seats over there."

Luckily she was able to take her seat and the sunshade before the May Queen procession had taken up places on the lawn. Joey, who had been flapping a vigorous fan, welcomed her enthusiastically. "I'm delighted to have a little shade," she observed. "Now we start the crowning."

Madge laughed as she looked across to where her youngest daughter was standing, very stately in her robes of white and long green mantle, borne by two of the Juniors. In front of her was Len, holding the May Queen's crown over her head. The crown descended on the fair curls. Len moved back and to one side and Ailie, very pretty and for once in her life looking shy, moved back to the flower-decked chair which served as a throne. It had been raised with three steps up to the final platform. Ailie, moving backwards, forgot this, tripped and fell full length with a yell which was echoed by quite half her court. Luckily Reg had followed Len to see the fun. He sprang forward, caught the queen before she was quite recumbent and steadied her on her feet, then, taking her hand in his, he very gravely handed her up the steps to the throne.

It was beautifully done and so quickly that quite half the audience were under the impression that it was part of the show. Ailie sat down and bowed very gravely to the young doctor, and Jo, who had seen the whole thing and knew exactly what had happened, was edified to hear a lady in front of her explaining to her next door neighbour that the School and the Sanatorium were run largely in conjunction with each other and that this had been the way chosen to show that to the audience.

Mary-Lou and Vi had also decided to watch Spring's effort. Jack Lambert and Jane Carew had taken charge of Bruno, so that the two old friends had no need to worry about him.

"He'll be all right with us," Jane said. "We can see that he has plenty of drinks and we'll keep him in the shade. This is no weather for dogs."

They had found seats well to the back but nowhere near Joey and Madge. They were watching the proceedings with deep interest when, as Ailie began her backward progress, Mary-Lou grabbed Vi's arm. "She's taken no notice of how she ought to go. She'll trip and fall. Oh, the little idiot!" She was for the moment a Chalet School prefect as she regarded with horror Ailie's backward movement.

She gave a gasp of relief as Reg Entwistle sprang forward and caught Ailie. "You know," she said later to Vi, "I rather think Reg will get what he wants. He's certainly got all his wits about him."

Vi, who had heard all the latest school gossip that Mary-Lou could hand on to her, nodded thoughtfully. "It seems peculiar that a girl who was merely a Middle when we were prefects should be considering marriage," she said in an elderly way, "but I suppose it has to come."

Whereupon Mary-Lou giggled.

After this, the sword dancers came and displayed Flamborough, which went down very well. The Morris dancers followed and the show ended with a Maypole dance.

"And now," said Jo, "have you made all your purchases?"

Madge nodded. "Yes, my purse is empty, and I don't know about you, but I want to have a shot at Tom Gay's competition."

"Oh, so do I," exclaimed Jo, "and when that is over I'm going in for the other competitions. I'll part with you here and you can

172

go and chat with your old friends while I amuse myself in my own way."

"What's that?" asked Madge, regarding her with suspicion. "Do remember, Jo, that you're the mother of the Head Girl."

"Not for much longer now," sighed Jo.

"No-o," said Madge thoughtfully, "but unless I am much mistaken your Head Girl daughter is going to be an engaged daughter before very long."

"I'm not so sure. Reg knows what he wants, but I'm not certain about Len, and I don't mind telling you that it's about the first time in her life that I haven't been sure. Reg is a dear boy, but—" and with that she departed, leaving her sister wishing it were possible to give her a good shaking on the spot.

Chapter XIV

GRAND TOTAL

LEN was hard at work in the office sorting out the takings up to date. Rosalie Dene was also there, and Ted Grantley, Eve Hurrell, Priscilla Dawbarn and two people from VIb—Ruey Richardson and Audrey Everett. The girls sorted the notes into hundred-franc packets, ten packets were then put up together and the thousand-franc bundles were placed in a safety box which was to be locked and put into the safe.

Three or four of the mistresses were assembled in the corridor outside, three or four more made a group outside the office window. There had been a good many burglaries in the area lately and the school was taking no chances.

"Although," said Nancy Wilmot, "how anyone would have the nerve to come burglaring here on a day like this is something I can't even imagine. Not only have we the entire school loose on the premises but there are all the visitors as well. It would be difficult, I imagine, for any would-be burglars to get away with it."

That was the general opinion. Jack Maynard pointed out that it was also possible for total strangers to come in unquestioned. "However, we must just do our best," he said.

Joey, having left her sister, went to enjoy herself over the Christmas doings displayed in the Winter episode. She paused to condole with Adrienne Rousselle, who was Father Christmas and bemoaning herself because of her warm robes. Jo's own Felicity was the Christmas Fairy. Jack Lambert came along with her to ask if Felicity might go round the grounds with her in the little minicar belonging to one of the staff and distribute sundry draw tickets.

"Don't ask me, ask the Head," said Joe. "Felicity's in her charge at the moment."

Miss Annersley laughed. "By all means so long as you don't upset the car and do anything drastic," she said pleasantly, while she glanced at her watch. "There's only another hour before we begin on the competition winners, so you had better make the most of your time."

Jack went off with Felicity clinging to her arm, and the Head and Mrs Maynard looked at each other and laughed.

"You know," said Joey, "Felicity is beginning to develop a fondness for Jack. She thinks she's marvellous and doesn't she know a lot! At least, that's what she said to me."

"I wish she did," Miss Annersley said in heartfelt tones. "Apart from maths, certain forms of science and mechanics, Jack is not what I should call a learned young person."

"No," said Jo with a grin, "but if things go on as they look like going on, Felicity is going to avenge Len over the questions business. You know how Len has always had to be ready to answer any sort of odd question Jack chose to fire at her. Well, now I can see Felicity playing that game with Jack. I wonder," she added meditatively, "how Jack is going to like it?"

That was something no one could tell them yet, so Jo went off to look at Tom's magnificent effort, and the Head was caught up by a bunch of Old Girls who all wanted to talk to her at once and in three different languages. Jo had just remarked aloud that the Inn was really suitable only for a museum when Miss Wilson's voice behind her said, "I couldn't agree more!" Jo spun round with an exclamation.

"Bill! I've hardly seen anything of you today. Where have you been putting yourself?"

Bill grinned. "Oh, here and there! Are you going in for the

competition, Jo? I am, although I can't think why; it wouldn't be any earthly use to me."

"But think of the kudos you'd get," Jo said with a wicked twinkle. "Of course I'm going in for it, but I shan't win it. There are too many names to choose from."

Bill agreed and they made their entries, and then went off together to enter for all the other competitions they could find, until finally the great Burmese gong which was rung for meals sounded out on the still hot air calling everyone in the grounds to the front of the house where Dr Jack was set to announcing the winners of various draws and competitions.

The enormous cake, made and presented by the Domestic Science Class, went to the Matron of the Sanatorium. A most beautifully-dressed doll which came from Nina Konstam, Odile Paulet and Henriette Zengal, three Swiss girls who were great friends, fell to the lot of Suzanne Mercier of Vb. Jack Lambert's sister Anne won a magnificent flask of eau-de-Cologne which had been presented by Frau Mieders. Sundry other prizes fell to visitors including a delightful Noah's Ark which had been made by two of the young doctors, and Val Pertwee of all people, won a charmingly fitted up work case which she regarded with jaundiced eyes.

"Now everyone will expect me to sew!" she said disgustedly.

Finally they came to Tom's effort.

Dr Maynard beamed round on everyone before announcing, "I will now unveil the sign of the Inn. No one, not even Miss Annersley, has yet seen it, so whatever it is will come as a surprise, I imagine, to everyone present." He stooped over the model and very carefully peeled off the paper which covered the inn sign. The important people who were near enough to see bent forward eagerly. Quite a number behind them stood on tiptoe and Joey, pitying those who couldn't possibly see anything, read aloud, "'The St George and Dragon'. Oh, and what a lovely sign! How did Tom get it?"

"Who on earth painted it?" Madge exclaimed.

Miss Annersley came forward. "I know everyone will want to see the sign," she said, her beautiful voice ringing out clearly over the murmurs. "I think the best plan will be if you will form into line and file slowly past so that you can all see it. As for who did it for Miss Gay, I can't tell you, but I will find out. But first of all—who has guessed it?"

Jack Maynard laughed. "Someone who has had very few prizes from the draws in our Sales, one of the School's foundation stones, and oddly enough, the only person to guess it—Matron Lloyd."

A cry came from the ranks of Inter V. "Matey's won it! Oh fabulous!" It was Jack Lambert's voice. Loud cheers followed. Matey was a favourite with everyone, although as more than one of her lambs had observed over the years, "a tongue that could take the skin off you, and if you knew what was good for you, you did what she told you without fuss and without argument."

Jack went to where she was standing, looking rather stunned. "Congratulations, Matey! I don't think I need tell you what the School feels about it. We shall have to find somewhere to put it. That bandbox of a room of yours will never hold it, but—"

By this time Matey had recovered from the shock to some extent. "Thank you," she said, "but no one need trouble to find a special room for it. It's joining the Elizabethan model in our museum, so that is settled."

Jack laughed. "You always did know your own mind. I may add that the hint about animals brought a positive farmyard, not to say zoo in ideas. We had bulls, lions of every colour, eagles, which I should hardly call animals myself, harts, deer, stags, and one bright person even suggested a wolf. Sundry dogs made their appearance, including greyhounds and talbots."

That was the end of the draws and the competitions, while Gaudenz and three of the other men came to carry off Matey's prize to the museum with Nancy Wilmot accompanying them to

177

unlock the door. Mary-Lou caught hold of Matron.

"What put you on to it, Matey?" she asked. "Nobody else seems to have thought of it."

Matron laughed. "Well, first of all we were told it was a typical English inn, and as far as that goes, no one was likely to argue about that. St George is the patron saint of England. When you think of England you think of him. And then the animal—well, what animal *does* one connect with St George? It was easy enough to work it out."

"I'm not so sure," Jo, who had been listening with interest, said. "Easy enough perhaps to work out St George. After all there must be hundreds of English inns dedicated to him. But the George and the Dragon—no, that's not so usual. You're a clever woman, Matey."

"Kindly stop being so childish, Jo. I needn't say how thrilled I am to have won such a prize, and I hope," she added, looking round at Miss Annersley and the dozen or so other mistresses who were standing near, "that I need not add that it belongs to the School, now and always."

That was practically the wind-up of the Sale, except that Reg proposed that they should have a Dutch Auction with all the oddments that were left and get rid of everything. This was received with acclamation. Not that anybody had much money left now, but at least it would clear the hobbies' cupboards of left overs and give them a chance to start afresh next term; besides adding to the funds. The visitors were quickly clearing off now, the little mountain train was carrying away many people, the School's own buses had also been called into service, and people who had come in their own cars were streaming down the motor road to the plain in a long procession.

Karen had prepared Kaffee und Kuchen for the Juniors, whose mistresses had them in charge and saw that they got a good meal before they were sent out to the playing fields to be out of the way. The Middles and the Seniors also had a light meal before they were turned on to clearing away all the trimmings of the stands; but before that happened quite a number of the girls were sent off to get rid of their dresses and put on their School uniform. All things considered, the paper frocks had stood up very well to the exigencies of the day, but quite a number were barely decent by this time.

John Peel, Santa Claus and various other warmly-clad people were thankful to change into cotton frocks and the Seasons were glad to be rid of their floating robes which had a trying habit of catching on to everything. The mistresses had plenty to do to see to all this, so as usual the reckoning up of the takings went to the prefects.

"I," said Mary-Lou, "am going to add up Bruno's takings. I shall be very interested to see how he has done." She clapped the gentleman's flank as he came up to her at the sound of his name. "Clever boy, Bruno! Much cleverer than Minette. She hasn't collected a penny."

"That's where you're wrong," Matey said. "Minette has collected fifty francs."

"What! How did she do it?" It was a chorus.

"Karen has sold two of her kittens for twenty-five francs each."

"But she couldn't possibly sell them yet. They're not a week old," protested Kathy Ferrars.

"No, but they're sold in advance, so to speak. They will stay with Mamma till they're five weeks old, and then go to their proper homes. It was Karen's idea, I may say. So you see Minette has a paw in the pudding as well as Bruno."

After this everybody turned on to adding up. It was not a very rapid business because some of the notes, being elderly, stuck, and others were badly crumpled and torn. But at last the worst was over. Notes had been bundled into piles of five hundred francs each and then carefully marked with the name of the stall from which the takings came, and so with the extras—competitions, draws and so on.

Mary-Lou, hard at work on the contents of the boxes from Bruno's harness, was the first to announce her total. She had called in Vi to help her, and looking up with flushed faces the pair announced triumphantly, "Bruno has taken seven hundred and ten francs!"

"I call that magnificent," Mary-Lou added. "Well done, Bruno!"

The next to reach its full total was Tom's English inn, and that really was outstanding, one thousand and five francs. The other stalls produced the usual amounts; Matey's jams and jellies always brought in a goodly sum, and the needlework made a great appeal to people who were interested in sewing of all kinds.

Len, meeting with Margot as they went to take lists to Miss Wilmot and Miss Ferrars, who were checking up on all results, gave her sister a grin.

"The stall that hasn't done so well as last year," she said pensively, "is the bric-à-brac."

Margot giggled. "Gosh! Do you remember that awful silver collection that Mum loaded on to it?"

"I thought I told you girls that I would not be called Mum," said Joey's voice behind them. "You may call me Mother, Mamma, and I don't mind Mater, but I will *not* be Mum! That understood?"

"Sorry," said Margot, crimson to the roots of her golden curls, "but it's short and easy."

"So are the other three," her mother informed her. "In any case I've told you I won't have it and that's enough."

Miss Annersley came up to them. "Well, how have we done so far?" she inquired.

"Well, except for the bric-à-brac stall, better than ever," Len said. "But of course last year we did have that awful silver set out that was one of Mamma's wedding presents. I can't imagine," she went on thoughtfully, "how anyone could ever choose such a thing. Truly, Mamma, it's the most ghastly affair I have ever seen in that line."

Joey laughed. "I know. It was originally a wedding present to the Stuffer's parents when they were married, and that, I imagine, was somewhere in the fifties of the last century. Taste in those days," she went on solemnly, "was *not* what it is today. Well, does anybody know what the sum total is?"

"Not yet," Len said. "I'm just taking some new lists to the office, but I think we haven't done too badly."

And indeed they hadn't. When the last totals from the competitions and stalls came in the gross sum for the Sale was a handsome one. By that time it was so late that it was decided to let things stand over until next week when they would have some idea of the expenditure and could put down the net result.

"To-morrow," said Miss Annersley, "we shall have a very quiet day to give everyone a chance of recovering from all the excitements of the past week. Anyone who wants to go to an early service at church may do so, otherwise you will go to an eleven o'clock service and in the afternoon you will all rest. Remember that the majority of you will have long journeys ahead of you, and we want to return you to your homes as quickly as possible."

And with this she left them, for the telephone had been ringing and Rosalie had appeared to summon her to answer it.

Chapter XV

THUNDERSTORM

OVERNIGHT the weather had changed, and the school woke to a grey day with a threat of rain.

"Thank goodness it's kept off till today," Margot remarked as she came back from Early Mass.

"If you ask me," Ted observed, "we're in for a storm. Just look at that sky!"

The half-dozen or so prefects who were crossing the playing fields from the School's little chapels paused for a moment to gaze up at the heavy sky. It was quite clear that a storm was in the offing. The clouds seemed almost to touch the tree tops. There was not a breath of wind. Con looked round uncomfortably.

"Well, my candid opinion," she said, "is that there'll be no church for anybody except ourselves. That sky means mischief."

Len glanced round to where the men were hard at work taking down the stands and wheeling them off. "I don't like it," she said, "and I think we'd better hurry up and get under cover *now*. Come along, folks. Get those Juniors together and walk them back as quickly as you can."

No sooner said than done. The Middles and the Juniors were lined up and marched off as fast as possible. However, they succeeded in reaching the school some time before the storm broke. Indeed, they were marching into the Speisesaal for Frühstück before the first flash of lightning gave them warning of what was likely to come. But when it came, it was sharp. There was a terrific glare as a sword of white light shot across the grey sky, to be followed almost immediately by a long heavy rumbling of thunder. One or two of the Juniors, who were nervous, and tired out by the previous day's efforts, cried out, and some of the small ones dissolved into tears. Luckily the matrons were accustomed to dealing with this sort of thing on occasion and so were the prefects, so that there were plenty of folk to comfort the nervous ones. Further, a few words from the Head to two of the young mistresses sent them scurrying to close the shutters and switch the lights on.

"Though what we shall do if the electricity goes off I just wouldn't know," Kathy Ferrars remarked to Peggy Burnett.

Matey, standing behind her, laughed. "Use candles, of course." She turned and looked down the long room. "Gretchen von Ahlen and Erica Standish, come with me to the storeroom. I will give you out candles. Priscilla Dawbarn and Primrose Trevoase, here are my keys. Open the third cupboard in the second storeroom and bring out the candlesticks you will find there. The following girls will put candles into them. Marie Angeot, Samaris Davies, Emmy Friedrich, Althea Glenyon, Barbara Craven, Carlotta von Eschenau and Ottillie Sneider. When you have finished that you will come back to your places at the table and we will have Frühstück."

The Head nodded to herself. Several of the girls Matey had named were nervous subjects; far better for them to be occupied and be given a chance to pull themselves together. The others took their seats and waited. Presently the entire band was there and although the thunder was now so loud and continuous that it was almost impossible to hear oneself speak, the girls were steady. As the last took her place the Head struck her bell on the high table. "Stand for grace," she said quietly. Everyone rose and the School's brief grace was repeated in Miss Annersley's beautiful voice, which somehow managed to pierce the noise of the thunder and reach everyone.

Then they sat down to the Sunday Frühstück of fruit and cream, accompanied by rolls and butter and black cherry jam. When they had finished they were marched off upstairs to perform dormitory duties. The matrons had summoned the maids to close the upstairs shutters, for the storm was raging. And now was to be seen the wisdom of Matron's candles. As the girls hurried upstairs every light in the place suddenly went out, but the candles were in the corridors, the prefects had matches and lit them at once; other candles were lit in the dormitories, and every dormitory prefect was on her toes to make sure that her own charges performed their duties without fooling about. It was very rarely the candles had to be used on the Görnetz Platz, but their usage was very carefully guarded.

"I wonder what we're going to do next," Val Pertwee murmured to her next door neighbour, as she beat up her pillows. "No church, of course."

"Don't you worry," Samaris Davies remarked from the opposite side of the room. "We shall probably have little private services of our own."

"Stop gossiping and hurry up and finish up here," said Jane Carew who was the dormitory prefect. "As soon as you've finished, line up at the door. The next thing is to march down to Hall." She stopped abruptly as a positively ear-splitting explosion broke overhead. "If this goes on," she yelled in an effort to make herself heard, "we shall all end with sore throats! What a storm!"

As if to emphasize her remark there came another crash and several people put their hands over their ears. Brigit Ingram looked positively scared.

"You might almost think—" she began, but what you might almost think remained unexplained as the thunder pealed forth again. By this time the last bed had been made and Jane, having lined the girls up, marched them off downstairs to Hall, where quite half of the School was already assembled.

And now they could hear the crash of rain coming full tilt.

"Do you think," asked Althea in awe-stricken tones, "that we shall have a flood?"

"Oh, almost certainly," Erica Standish replied cheerfully. "Gosh! I wonder if this will set the spring in the hollow that was started last summer going again?"

"I hope not." Pricilla Dawbarn's voice sounded from the doorway. "We can't afford to lose any more cricket ground, you know."

"Oh, mon Dieu!" exclaimed Adrienne Desmoines, horror in her voice. "Suppose the tennis courts were affected? What should we do then?"

Len, who had come in in time to hear this, answered her, "In any case, my dear, it wouldn't matter so frightfully much at the moment. Don't forget we go home on Wednesday."

"Oh, gloryanna, so we do!" cried Flavia Ansell, otherwise known as Copper. "There's been so much happening that I'd forgotten the holidays were on us."

By this time the entire School was assembled in Hall. Miss Lawrence was seated at the piano with half a dozen of the School orchestra assembled round her. The Head and the rest of the staff were on the dais, among them, to everyone's surprise, Mr Denny the singing master. He came forward.

"We will now have a little choral work," he said. "We will begin with Schubert's setting of the twenty-third psalm. Will the choir please assemble in their right places."

The girls who belonged to the choir hurriedly took their places and the rest crowded back on to the spare forms. Miss Lawrence, who had been watching Mr Denny's baton closely, struck a chord; up went the baton and the choir broke into Schubert's lovely setting. This was followed by a very favourite hymn, "Oh Worship the King," which everyone knew. Then came Bach's arrangement for "Sheep may safely graze", and then once more hymns for the entire school.

Nancy Wilmot slipped out halfway through and came back with a look on her face which brought Miss Annersley to the door where the mistress had paused.

"What is it, Nancy?" she asked anxiously.

"A lovely flood," Nancy said resignedly.

"Oh *dear*!" said Miss Annersley. "Just what I was afraid of." She looked across to where the staff were singing lustily, caught Rosalie Dene's eye and beckoned to her to leave Hall. "Rosalie, you had better ring up the station first, and see what news they have for us. Then, get the Sanatorium. I can't say I like the sound of this at all."

"I don't like it myself," Rosalie said ruefully. "I suppose if the worst came to the worst we could always go over the mountain through the woods, but that would mean having to send all the girls' luggage after them, even if we succeeded in getting them safely to the other side."

"And," put in Nancy with a cheerful grin which made Miss Annersley long to shake her, "how do we know what's been happening on the other side of the mountain?"

"We don't," the Head said curtly, "and I may as well inform you that if it comes to that it will mean that it's an emergency. Don't forget that we are bound to be short on food supplies at the very end of term, and if we're flooded out so is everyone else up here."

"Oh well," said Nancy resignedly, "there are worse troubles at sea." The Head regarded her furiously but said nothing, and Miss Wilmot had the sense to let it go.

Gaudenz arrived at that point with the information that they were cut off from the valley for the present at any rate. The water had got into the railway generators and everything on the railroad was held up. But worse was to follow.

Rosalie Dene came hurrying from the office. "I've rung the railway and there are no trains at present, something to do with the electricity having gone off. Then I rang the San. They've been flooded round about but they say it's going down. But they're very worried. Sir James Russell and Dr Maynard are both at Freudesheim, were there last night, and worse than that, Reg Entwistle was called out early this morning to attend an accident case. He got there all right and left, but nobody has seen anything of him since. They've rung the Maynards and told them, but of course at present no one can get through from there to the San." Her eyes were horror-stricken as she looked at the Head. "What ought we to do about this latest news?"

"First of all, keep it to ourselves," Miss Annersley said sharply. "Don't let anybody else hear a murmur of it. Secondly, the girls have had singing for long enough. Get all the jigsaw puzzles out and share them out among the younger ones. Put the prefects in charge. Oh, dear, why did this have to happen on a Sunday? People who don't want to do jigsaws may read. Yes, I know all the library books have been collected and checked but this is the sort of emergency that occurs once in a lifetime. We must keep those girls occupied somehow. Where's Jo? She can put her brains in steep and help us out. Rosalie, ring up Freudesheim and when you've got Jo, let me know."

Rosalie went off. "What an ending to term!" observed Nancy. "It only wants that her nursery has started whooping cough or chicken pox or something of that nature to put the lid on everything."

Jo's nursery had no intention of doing any such thing. Instead they had been keeping everyone on edge with a series of antics that had never been bettered in Freudesheim. Geoff, the youngest of Jo's boys and twin to little Phil, was as full of mischief as his next brother Michael, and on this occasion he was rather more so. He had sneaked down to the kitchen, collected a large tin tray which was one of the treasures of Anna's heart and inaugurated a sledging game on the stairs leading from the back attics to the bathroom landing. It was a beautiful game but it had a sad ending. Geoff, mercifully by himself on the tray, steered it into the railings, where one railing happened to be weak. Crash! went the tray. Crash! went the railing, taking with it three others, and Geoff, yelling at the top of his voice, was tossed down the well of the stairs to land on his father's chest, flooring that gentleman completely.

Between Geoff's yells, to which were added those of his twin, Jack's outburst of strong language when he had recovered his breath, and Jo's shrieks of dismay, Madge Russell was unable to make herself heard and Sir James Russell, coming downstairs from an extra "lie in", was so overcome that he did nothing but roar with laughter, since nobody had been badly hurt, not even Jack who was winded, or Geoff who was more frightened than damaged. As for Jo, once she was assured that nothing ailed either her husband or her offspring, she nearly went into hysterics with laughter.

Mary-Lou, who had been sitting in the salon mending a ladder which had appeared in one stocking, heard the noise and came flying to find out what had happened. When she heard Joey's vivid description she went off into peals of laughter.

"I'm sorry," she said in response to Jo's vehement protest, "but honestly whatever sort of a childhood did you have to merit such a collection of sinners in your family?"

Jo was unable to reply, since at that juncture the storm broke, startling everyone nearly out of their wits. Thanks to Geoff's prank they had never noticed its approach, so the flash of lightning with which it opened not only startled them but scared the tinies badly.

The school heard nothing about this episode until much later, because by the time Rosalie rang Jo to say Miss Annersley wanted to speak to her, the storm was over and the news that Reg was missing had reached Freudesheim and driven everything else out of her head.

Jo was horrified at the news. Apart from anything there might be between Reg and Len, she and Jack had looked after the young doctor in many ways from his schooldays up to his appointment as one of the assistant doctors at the San.

"But where can he be?" she cried. "Oh Hilda, I don't like this!"

"Neither do I," snapped Miss Annersley, "but at the moment I don't see what can be done about it."

Jem Russell, who had been listening in to this, now intervened. "We can't leave it at that," he said brusquely. "Goodness only knows where he may be stranded. No, Joey, don't talk, let me think."

Joey looked at him. "Hurry up and think to purpose," she commanded. "How are we going to look for him when the whole Platz is knee deep in water?"

"Aren't there any stilts around?" Jem asked.

"Three or four pairs," Joey said eagerly. "That's an idea, Jem."

Miss Annersley broke in. "Well, I can tell you one thing. He was called out to that shelf beyond the brook. He must have found that he couldn't get the car through the flood because it has been found above the stone bridge. One of the men has just come in with that information. He had taken his case out because it's not there, so we do know that much."

"Well, if it's beyond the brook," Joey said thoughtfully, "did he go up or down?"

"Your guess is as good as mine," the Head said. "I'm sending Gaudenz and Andry to hunt around there. Whether they can cross I don't know. We can but try."

"Well, I'll give you a tip," said Jo. "Hunt up any stilts the School has and send the men along on them. It will make it easier."

"Don't worry," her friend told her tartly, "Gaudenz has thought of that one already."

"You haven't told Len, have you? Keep it from her at all costs until we know what's happened."

"Give me credit for a *little* sense, can't you?"

"Oh yes, I can give *you* credit for common sense, but what about the grape-vine?"

"We can only do our best, and," Miss Annersley said slowly, "I'm not so sure that after all it mightn't be as well for Len to be faced with anxiety of this kind. She's eighteen, nearly nineteen, and it's time she grew up. I wouldn't give her a shock like this if it could be avoided, but can it?"

At which point she rang off and when an infuriated Jo tried to get her again the School telephone was in use elsewhere.

As it turned out Len already knew that Reg was missing. One of the maids had told her. It was a nasty shock but she had plenty of self-control. She went white but she kept her head. "Miggi," she said severely, "don't repeat that sort of gossip. It *is* just gossip, and you could get into trouble for spreading it. Now remember what I say, or I must speak to Karen."

That was quite enough for Miggi. She hurriedly promised not to say a word and once she was assured of that Len left her and went as fast as she could to the Head's study.

"Auntie Hilda," she cried as she burst in, "what's the truth about Reg?"

The Head looked at her quickly. "So you've heard! The truth is that nobody knows quite what has happened. His car is parked up among the pines above the stone bridge, he himself has gone with his case, and that is all I can tell you at the moment."

"You don't think anything's happened—" Len's voice shook.

"I don't think so. What is much more likely is that he's stranded somewhere and is waiting for someone to come and rescue him."

"Do you really think that?"

"Yes, I do. Now will you please go and collect some of the Seniors and tell them to lay the tables for Mittagessen."

"But Auntie Hilda—"

"I'm sorry, Len, that is all I have to say to you now," and Len had to go, realizing with sudden shock that whatever she may have felt yesterday, today was a different matter, and she would have given almost anything to know that Reg was safe.

It was a very horrible morning for poor Len, but just as they were marching into the Speisesaal for Mittagessen Jem turned up with news. Reg had slipped in crossing the heavily swollen brook and struck his back against a submerged boulder. He had contrived to struggle to the bank but there he had collapsed and Jem, who had been one of the party who had found him, had been thankful to get him to Freudesheim, a matter of great difficulty, where he was put to bed.

"Is he badly hurt?" Miss Annersley asked anxiously.

"Not so far as I can judge. The spine is bruised and one shoulder badly strained. We can say nothing definite until we see an X-ray. In the meantime it should settle things for him and Len. I'm hoping so, anyway."

Chapter XVI

UP THE CHALET SCHOOL!

"How are you going to get Reg back to San?" Len demanded of her uncle. Without asking permission she had charged after him and Miss Annersley when they went into the Annexe.

"We can't do anything until the water has gone down considerably."

"Why not? You got him here! And when can I see him?"

"Well, not at present. In fact—" Jem gave Miss Annersley a twinkling look, "I don't know what you're doing in this room at all. I thought you were supposed to be having Mittagessen."

Miss Annersley was more tender-hearted than he was. "That is quite all right, Len," she said quietly, "but as at present Reg is not to be allowed any visitors, I think your uncle is right and you had better go and take charge of your table."

"I *can't*! Not till I know how Reg is."

"Then you're going to go very hungry," her uncle told her with a grin. "Pull yourself together, Len. At the moment Reg is semi-conscious and likely to remain so for the next hour or two. As soon as he can recognize anybody you shall be his first visitor. But just at present get on with your proper job."

Len flushed. "I see. You promise me that I shall see him as soon as possible?"

He nodded. "Word of honour. Now that's settled, off you go."

Len departed, only half satisfied. As a matter of fact it was not until eleven hours that she was summoned to Miss Annersley's salon, told to get into her outdoor things and taken across to Freudesheim by Nancy Wilmot and left to her mother's care.

Joey went straight to the point. "Is it the real thing, Len?"

Len nodded. "Yes, I found that out when Reg went missing. I don't want to be married yet. I want my college course. A degree is a useful sort of thing to have, particularly in these days. Once I've got that if Reg still wants me then I'm his."

"What do you mean exactly by that?" Jo demanded. Then she added, "Mind you, Len! You're not going on playing fast and loose with that poor boy."

"I don't mean to," Len said. "If nothing else will satisfy him, I'll be engaged. But I won't be married at once."

"I should think not!" her mother exclaimed. "You don't get married until you've graduated and that's that!"

"All right, that's understood. And now, Mamma, *please* let me see him."

"Upstairs in Margot's old room."

"Thank you." Len departed at speed and Joey looked at her brother-in-law.

"Well, that's Len settled, I suppose," she said with a sigh. "Margot is also settled. I suppose Con will be next. Oh, *why* do children have to grow up?"

"Yes, we've had that experience, too," he told her. "Sybs and Josette both married, only Ailie of the girls left at school; but it's got to come, so pull yourself together, woman. Now I'm going to the telephone. I must find out what the road is like from here to the San."

Meanwhile upstairs Len had entered the room where Reg, very sore and aching, was lying. As she appeared round the door he looked at her with startled eyes. "Len!" he said incredulously.

She went very pink. "Reg!" she said. "Oh, you poor dear, how dreadful you look! Are you badly hurt?"

"I don't think so," he returned. "Merely wrench and strain." Then as she came up to the bed he caught her hands. "Does this mean—"

193

Len nodded. "I suppose so. Yes!"

Reg pulled her to him and Len sank down beside the bed. His arms went round her, then he held her from him and looked at her searchingly.

"I take it we're engaged. Like it, darling?"

Len chuckled. "So much I can't think why I didn't know it before. It all seems absolutely natural and *very* nice! Yes, of course we're engaged, only it *must* be kept dark until term ends."

As the elders all agreed with this there was no argument about it. Apart from her sisters, Mary-Lou, and Ruey Richardson who was counted as one of the Maynard family, the only person who was told was Ted. Small Felicity was not told; as Con remarked, "You know what kids are!"

On the Monday the school finished its packing and general tidying up. By this time the waters had subsided very considerably, the motor road was clear except for puddles in the ruts, but what did rather alarm people was the way the hollow which had appeared the previous year owing to a landslide had deepened. As this was in what had once been one of the School's cricket pitches and was on the edge of the School land very near to the motor road, there was some anxiety as to whether the said dip might not become worse, even to continuing across the motor road to the edge of the cliff on the other side. It was decided that there must be a meeting of everyone concerned to discuss whether a new highroad should be built to run behind the School or the present one restored.

Another trouble was that quite a number of pines had fallen under the force of the water down the mountain slope to the valley below. Some of these were lying across the mountain railway track, and though the men would be up next day to remove the tree trunks it was likely to be a slow business, what with the blockage on the line and the water that had got into the generators.

"Well," Ted remarked in the prefects' room that evening,

"we've had some happenings during the term before now, but I must say I think this term beats everything."

"What else did you expect?" Margot demanded. "You might have known that the term *we* finished would end up with fireworks."

"Fireworks? Don't you mean waterworks?" Priscilla Dawbarn said with a chuckle.

"Well, waterworks if you like," Margot said with a grin. "At any rate let us say that we are making a splash! Now that *is* true. There goes the bell for Prayers. Then I suppose we must see to getting the Juniors off to bed. What with one thing and another they'll be arriving home for the holidays in a half-dead condition."

"To-morrow," Audrey Everett remarked, "I propose to keep the Middles occupied with tennis, and on Wednesday we depart."

"Do you indeed! How will you get down to the plain? Because I don't think the railway will be usable even then. Quite a length of line has been swept away." This was Priscilla Dawbarn. "I rather think it's going to mean the coaches, and what is the road like to the west? We know what it's like at this end! What about the other?"

"I should imagine it will be fairly clear by that time," Carmela said thoughtfully. "At any rate we can't do anything about it at the moment. And now, come on to Prayers. Goodness knows what the Middles are up to left to themselves like this."

The prefects streamed along to Hall, where they separated into their two bodies, the Protestants taking over the top end which held the big dais, and the Catholics taking the lower end for themselves, while Miss Burnett, Miss Ferrars and Miss Wilmot saw to the closing of the folding doors which divided the great room into two parts.

Once Prayers were ended the Juniors and the Junior Middles were packed off to bed, while the rest of the school set the forms back against the walls and enjoyed an hour's dancing, after which they all went up to bed.

"And to-morrow," observed Samaris Davies, "we shall all have cleared off. Mustn't the School feel empty?"

After all the excitement of the past two or three days the night proved to be tranquil. The school at large slumbered sweetly, but it meant rising early next day. Frühstück was at 7.30 and a body of very busy gentlemen were arriving from Berne for a preliminary inspection of that truly alarming dip in what had once been a cricket pitch. They were expected about ten o'clock; nobody wanted the Juniors and Junior Middles about the place when they arrived, so the Head organized sundry walks which took them up into the woods, well out of the way of the experts. The Senior Middles were set on to packing up the sports paraphernalia and the Seniors, apart from the prefects who were in charge of walks, were fully occupied in checking up on the remaining goods such as flour, sugar, salt and so on in the Domestic Science kitchen.

Con Maynard collected a dozen members of the two Fifths and requested them to see that the library books taken out on the Sunday were all returned to the library in their proper places. In fact, the morning was fully occupied.

In the afternoon Mr Denny arrived and took the usual singing classes. He completely ignored the fact that this was the last possible working day of term and started the school off on a series of new songs.

"Honestly," exclaimed Margot, "Plato gets madder and madder with the years. Fancy starting us off on new songs the very last day of term."

"What annoys *me*," observed Con, "is that he's started us off on a really delightful song, but *we* shan't see the end of it."

"Oh, don't talk of it," exclaimed Primrose. "I simply hate to feel that this is the last of my schooldays, and goodness knows when our crowd will meet again."

"Oh, I daresay there'll be an Old Girls Day next summer," Ted Grantley said laughing.

"Yes. That may be," Carmela pointed out, "but many of us may not be able to attend."

"We must hope for the best," Audrey Everett remarked. "You never know your luck." At which point the gong sounded for Kaffee und Kuchen and they had to go downstairs to take charge of the various tables.

After that, time seemed to fly. The formrooms looked bare and stripped, for all vases and other adornments had been packed away in the cupboards. Bookshelves were severely straightened. The pictures had all been taken down, cleaned and packed into one of the cupboards in the stockroom, and by the time all that had been done it was time for Abendessen. Prayers came next, followed by bed for everyone under fifteen. The prefects and the two Sixth Forms met in Hall shortly before twenty-one hours.

"Well," said Len, "this will be good-bye for quite a lot of us. But remember, everybody, that there will always be a welcome for you up here, and that whatever else you may do, what you may become, you are Chalet School. That's all I have to say. But I wanted to say it now, because some of us leave so early to-morrow and you know what it's like on the last morning."

Ted Grantley grinned at her. "We do indeed, and you may be certain that we shall not forget, whatever happens. Even," she added with a sudden, wicked grin at Len, "though some of us may be married women with daughters of our own to become members of the Chalet School."

It was left to Con to wind up the meeting. "It's our School. We may leave; School will go on, and we shall still belong to it."

Margot jumped on to a nearby chair. "Everyone," she cried. "Up the Chalet School!"

And with one voice they joined in her exclamation, "Up the Chalet School!"

APPENDIX I: ERRORS IN THE FIRST EDITION

As Ruth Jolly comments in Appendix II, *Prefects* is peculiarly rich in EBDisms: girls flit from form to form, and their ages change; characters appear to be in two places at once; sentences are garbled, and adjacent paragraphs contradict each other. In this appendix we do not try to address, let alone resolve, such issues, but concentrate exclusively on obvious and apparent typographical errors and, where appropriate, their resolution. And as usual we have made no attempt to correct EBD's French and German.

PUNCTUATION

Always idiosyncratic, EBD's punctuation—in particular her use of commas—is even more wayward in *Prefects*, and all we have done is correct obvious typos. Missing opening and/or closing quotation marks have been inserted, and extraneous ones deleted; missing full stops have been added, while those which should clearly be commas, exclamation marks, colons or question marks have been changed, and vice versa. Misplaced or missing apostrophes have also been corrected. On the original Contents Page the title of the final chapter is 'Up the Chalet School'; this style is also used for the running heads, but the heading to the actual chapter ends with an exclamation mark. We have not attempted to standardise this and instead have followed the style exactly.

TRANSPOSITION

On page 184, in the penultimate line of the first paragraph, we have corrected 'the candles had be to used'.

CAPITALISATION

Where possible we have rationalised capitals so that majority usage is followed—eg 'Prayers', not 'prayers', when the corporate act is referred to, as the former appears much more frequently, and 'Sanatorium', not 'sanatorium', when the institution (as opposed to the school san) is meant—but in the case of 'school' or 'School', and of compounds thereof such as 'Senior school' and 'Junior School', this has not been possible as there are too many variables in context and meaning. We have also corrected any capitals which appear in the body of a sentence.

HYPHENATION

Again, we have rationalised hyphenated words to match the more usual form; we have not been able to do this where there is no majority usage, so we have left them: door-handle/ doorhandle/door handle; hymn-books/hymnbooks; and timetable/ time-table.

SPELLINGS

We have corrected obvious typos—bric-à-bac, broderie anglais, cencentrate, harnesss, lecide, and you're guess—and have inserted missing letters, for example in 'Cakes and Sweet[s] Stalls' (p143, paragraph 2, line 2). On page 170, in line 2 of the penultimate paragraph, it is clear that 'those' rather than 'these' is meant, and similarly on page 184, in line 4 of paragraph 4, 'positively' rather than 'positive'. Where there are variants we have once again standardised on majority usage—Inter V, not Inter Fifth, and Sixth, not VI [form]; many of them are sometimes compounds, sometimes not, such as 'halfway/half way'. Where there is no majority we have left them, so we have 'banisters/bannisters', 'etc/etc.', 'Games Fund/Funds' and 'fidgeted/fidgetted'.

NAMES

We have made all names consistent within the book, according to majority usage, as shown below:

Angeot, not Angout
Anna [Joey's helper], not Anne
Craven, not Cravon
Duffin, not Duffy
Grunbaum, not Grünbaum
Hurrell, not Hurrel
Mary-Lou, not Mary Lou
Mdlle, not Mddle
Ted, not Ten
Trevoase, not Trevoise

We have *not* corrected those which are different in other titles but consistent in *Prefects*, and we have left those where there is no majority usage (Engels/Engles, Wistaria/Wisteria). On page 175, in line 1 of paragraph 2, we do not know if 'Joe' should be 'Jo' or 'Joey' so we have left it.

INCORRECT REFERENCES

Page 87, paragraph 2, lines 4–5: 'Lo, hear, the gentle lark' should be 'Lo! Here the gentle lark'.
Page 156, penultimate paragraph, lines 1–2: 'like the walrus' should be 'like the carpenter'—the quotation is '"I doubt it," said the Carpenter,/and shed a bitter tear.'

Page 170, paragraph 9, line 6: 'Britain' should be 'the United Kingdom' or 'the British Isles'—Ireland is not part of Britain.
Page 185, last paragraph, lines 5–6: 'Oh Worship the King' should be 'O Worship the King' (this may just be a typo).

Laura Hicks, with gratitude to Adrianne Fitzpatrick and Ruth Jolly who spotted many of these
2007

APPENDIX II: *PREFECTS*—DOES IT REALLY BELONG?

Prefects is very much a 'last book'. Its place in the series remains assured, because it so neatly rounds off the story which begins with Joey as first pupil, and ends with her triplets' final term. It also settles once and for all the question of the triplets' future, with Len all set to marry Reg—although, unlike her mother, she will get her degree first; Con following in Joey's footsteps as an author; and Margot at last firmly settled in her vocation to become a nun. But nobody could claim that the book is entirely satisfactory. Although EBD is famous for her inconsistencies and non sequiturs, in *Prefects* they hit an all-time high; and the best that can be said for the plot is that we do see the triplets working together in leadership. That apart, there really *is* no plot, just two rather unrelated sections: the first five chapters are taken up with the entirely abortive motor-boat rebellion, and the remainder of the book is vaguely about the Sale, with a rather unlikely riot-cum-kidnapping thrown in for good measure. (Please, somebody, tell me how—and *why*—Mary-Lou hitched a lift to the Platz with the police late at night!)

It is fascinating to speculate on how much of the book is Elinor's own work. My own first thoughts tended towards the view that the two disparate sections might be by different authors. Like Aunt Luce, I have 'swithered' between two possibilities: did Elinor write the motor-boat rebellion, getting more and more bogged down as she tried to manufacture a really dangerous uprising among the Senior Middles from a situation so improbable that they really need only have been told 'No'? Or was this first part of the book perhaps 'ghosted' from some jotting of hers, and had EBD herself only got as far as continuing the story of the Sale, the plans for which were well under way in *Althea*?

We know that the contract for this book was signed only days before Elinor's death, and that she had been becoming increasingly frail. It might have seemed to Phyllis and Sidney Matthewman that there was a race against time to get the series completed. If the manuscript that Elinor had produced appeared unacceptably short, might Phyllis have taken it upon herself to add the opening episode—from a draft of Elinor's, naturally—to make publication viable? It seems strangely unlike EBD to have to fall back on illness to resolve Jocelyn's disgruntlement over being refused the boats; and why was Joey called in, since her advice, received initially with such acclaim, was in fact entirely ignored by a Miss Annersley who, in the event, simply makes the girls look foolish in public? If this was written by EBD, we would certainly expect Joey to save the day.

Perhaps, however, as Helen McClelland suggests in her introductory article, it's not a case of two sections by different authors, but rather a whole book written to some degree collaboratively. The apparent partition between the motor-boat theme and the Sale section might simply be because the rebellion idea had petered out. Or there could have been a break in the writing of the book, if Elinor was tired or in poor health. Certainly the Sale part of the story gives some grounds for supposing either that more than one hand was at work, or that the writing was done intermittently, since for example the girls spend the whole of Chapter X putting goods on the stalls (which apparently are out of doors as usual) for Saturday's Sale, and then in Chapter XI it is still only Wednesday!

Poor continuity, of course, is not in itself unlike EBD; she has famous muddles in many of her books, even if this is an extreme case. Much more striking, to my mind, is the atypical characterisation, particularly of Miss Annersley. In what other book is she ever so short-tempered—or anxious? "'Joey!" hissed Miss Annersley in an agitated whisper. "Get that dog away." ... Miss

Annersley glared at Jo …' (p163) Again, when Jo is worried sick about Reg's whereabouts during the flood: '"Neither do I," snapped Miss Annersley, "but at the moment I don't see what can be done about it."' (p189) And her reaction to Jocelyn and Co's proposed midnight picnic—'"You were *what*?" Miss Annersley almost gasped.' (p122)—seems rather extreme, considering that this is not the first time that such a thing has occurred under her jurisdiction! She doesn't always sound like herself in other situations, either, witness her request 'Well, go on and give us the hanes.' (p160)—an expression frequently used by Joey, and occasionally by Mary-Lou and Co, but never before by Miss Annersley.

Nor is the Head the only person to speak out of character. Joey, too, jumps quite uncharacteristically down Len's throat: '"What do you mean exactly by that?" Jo demanded. Then she added, "Mind you, Len! You're not going on playing fast and loose with that poor boy."' (p193) This after earlier expressing her own mixed feelings over the possible romance. Consider also Madge Russell's extraordinary remark on page 160: '"Hilda Annersley, have you suddenly gone dumb? Where would Jo be?"' However many years Madge may have spent in Canada in the past, one cannot really imagine EBD attributing to her such an Americanism as 'dumb' in the sense of 'unintelligent'. And while I can just about imagine Melanie calling Jo 'Auntie Joey', why on *earth* does Eve Hurrell do so (p140)?

There are occasions, too, when the girls show a singular lack of respect for the staff. '"Plenty of water in the Splashery," Primrose informed her with a grin.'—but she is speaking to Miss Burnett (p135)! And it is hardly tactful of Len to give the Head such a blatant vote of no confidence as '"If you've got Mamma on it I can see a hope. What has she suggested?"'! (p76)

In addition to those times when characters make inappropriate remarks, there seems sometimes to be some confusion as to who speaks which language, as in the following speech: "'Well, someone presented me with a bottle of green which I presume will act as a background. When that's done, then I shall refer to another colour. I've got pink here but I should also like some yellow. Audrey, what about a spot of yellow?'" (p138) The construction and choice of words here sound definitely foreign, but the speaker is Connie Winter, surely a native English speaker.

In fact the dialogue overall is well below EBD's usually high standard. For ultimate turgidity, commend me to the discussion about Sale goods on pages 133–4!

"Can if you like," Len said. "It might save trouble."

"Right. Then that's what we'll do."

"And now the next thing," said Ted. "There's all this pile of jigsaw puzzles. Where do we put them? With the books or in a heap by themselves?"

"Oh, I think by themselves," Margot said thoughtfully. "That'll give a neat pile one corner of the stall, and they all have to be priced separately. You'd better see to that, Priscilla. And Carmela—there are all those strings of beads that seem to have come in from nowhere that I can tell. They've just arrived."

"And very nice, too," said Eve with a grin. "They're none of them valuable, are they? Or *are* they?" she added thoughtfully, picking up a string.

"Had we better get someone who knows on to them?" Primrose asked.

"Well, *myself* I think they are mainly just beads," Priscilla remarked. "Not worth more than a few francs. We might hang them up on a long bar. They'll appeal to the kids, anyhow."

"Right. Well, that's settled," Jeanne Daudet observed.

Primrose cocked her head on one side. "Good! Then shall we get cracking on this lot?"

"Well, it would be something attempted, something done," Con observed.

"Right. Then let's get down to it," Eve said.

The book also contains a number of phrases and usages which seem not to appear anywhere else in the series. This is surprising, since it might be expected that EBD's active vocabulary would diminish as writing became more of a chore with age and illness, rather than that new words and phrases would be introduced. Examples are 'to have your idea cut at like that' (p49); 'quick in the uptake' (p145); 'tapped her lips' (p67); and 'Thus said Ted Grantley' (p217)—this last sounds like an *attempt* to be EBD; EBD's favoured construction would have read 'Thus Ted Grantley'.

Without possessing any of the specialist computer equipment referred to by Helen in her article, I have nonetheless amused myself by gathering a few statistics. (Details of my word counts may be found in Appendix III.) I mentioned above Miss Annersley's somewhat excessive dismay in response to the projected midnight picnic. Where else in the series, I asked myself, does the Head ever forget herself so far as to gasp? The answer is that in the course of the 59 other books Miss Annersley gasps only nine times, approximately one book in six, and never more than once in a book. In *Prefects*, she *almost* gasps once, and *actually* gasps twice more; this despite the fact that the book contains a total of only six gasps, of which half are therefore hers. In *Richenda*, at the other extreme, 22 gasps are recorded, none of them perpetrated by the Abbess. (In fact, *Jo of* holds the record, at 27 gasps, but Miss Annersley was not at the school then, so it doesn't really count!) At the very least we can say that in *Prefects* the Head—or perhaps EBD herself—was on a rather short fuse.

It was suggested to me that the frequency of use of a totally unimportant word might provide some interesting data, since if another author was involved this is the sort of pattern which might change. So I have further entertained myself by analysing the percentage occurrence of the word 'the' in the last ten books of the series. I wouldn't want to place too much weight on this very limited research, but it is a fact that, whereas the average percentage occurrence over the ten books is 4.74, in *Althea* it is 5.23 and in *Prefects* 5.41—the only two to be over 5 per cent, and the very two books singled out by Helen McClelland as feeling different from the rest of the series.

I also sought to confirm or refute an impression I had gained that in this book Con plays an unprecedentedly large part in leadership, while Len fades rather into the background—as though *someone* was tired of Len and wanted to give Con a chance. What I discovered on this occasion was entirely inconclusive. I analysed the last ten books in the series, and discovered that, in every case bar one, Len's name has the lion's share of mentions. Con and Margot are generally approximately on a level with each other. The exception is *Challenge*, where Margot leaps ahead with 127 mentions to Len's 118, while Con is well in the rear with only 38. In *Prefects*, contrary to my impression, Len is named 207 times, Con and Margot only 76 times each. So if Con does step forward it can only be in nature, not frequency, of appearance.

A quick skim of the story does give some support for my impression. In *Althea*, Con is still 'dreamy Con'; but as early as page 41 of *Prefects*, and again on page 43, we find her usurping the chairman's role at a prefects' meeting. On page 46 we actually find Len leaning on Con for support over the Middles' rebellion. On page 101 Con is seen bossing Len around, and on page 112 even the girls are astounded by her stentorian tones and Matey-like glare! She betters Matron Duffin's response to a domestic crisis, and on page 140 she takes charge in a cookery disaster, and apparently has things sorted in no time at all. On page 162 she is to be found marshalling the prefects—and on page 197 it falls to Con to wind up the story.

Moving away from numbers and back to words, I was struck by the tedious and artificial insistence on the role of the prefects, which reads rather as though someone had gone through and 'justified' the title of the book at regular intervals—'It was thanks to this sort of thing from the prefects that there was no panic among the girls' (p153)—but actually Margot has simply been snappily repressive! '[Mary-Lou] was for the moment a Chalet School prefect as she regarded with horror Ailie's backward movement.' (p172) '… as usual the reckoning up of the takings went to the prefects.' (p179)

More significant than any of these to my mind, however, is the unprecedented fact that milk is not mentioned anywhere in this book! When you consider how milk is forced upon the girls in season and out of season—they drink it, rich and creamy, to counteract the threat of TB; they have it cold with biscuits at Break, and hot to ward off chills after night-time misdemeanours; their breakfast coffee is notoriously full of the stuff; they even have it in their flasks on rambles (*A Chalet Girl from Kenya*, p51 Chambers edition, p74 GGBP)—this really seems an extraordinary omission.

If all these indications are taken together, it does seem likely that another hand than EBD's was at work in this book. But no one could really suppose that it was entirely 'ghosted'. In addition to the alien turns of phrase, there are some which are entirely characteristic. '"What's the why of that?"' cries Audrey Everett in the opening paragraph. Ted Grantley, throughout this book, is completely and convincingly herself—see for example page 156, where Louise Grunbaum is waxing sentimental about leaving school: 'Ted Grantley grinned at her. "Like the walrus, I shed a bitter tear. Come off it, Louise! You never know what might happen, and in any case, this is not the time to be morbid."'; and the scene where Matey donates the English Inn to the school is also exactly right: Matey at her most crisp and assertive, with her heart of gold shining through her best attempts to disguise it.

What could be more typical of Elinor than the description of picnic food on page 88:

> There were fresh rolls thickly buttered and sandwiched with slices of savoury meat and lettuce; hard-boiled eggs to eat with them; cartons of strawberries, sugared and creamed; to top up, a large slice each of Karen's special cake.

Mouth-watering! And despite Miss Annersley's unusual ill-humour, Bruno's stealing of the show at the opening of the Sale is a delight, as is Joey's 'complacent smile' when he gets away with it! Nor will I soon forget Jocelyn Marvell's extremely descriptive remark: "'It was an *unsweetened rice pudding* of a time".' (p131) Surely these are glimpses of EBD at her best, however submerged in less satisfactory verbiage they may be.

One author or two? It could be that some of the stylistic differences are simply attributable to old age and failing health. Or maybe Phyllis Matthewman really did play a significant role in the writing of *Prefects*. We will never know, but it is fun to speculate, and at least we were not left dangling halfway through the final term; the loose ends have all been tied up, and the Chalet School series is complete.

Ruth Jolly
2007

APPENDIX III: WORD COUNTS IN *PREFECTS OF THE CHALET SCHOOL*

GASP: FREQUENCY THROUGHOUT THE SERIES

Number	Book	Word count (approx)	Mentions of 'gasp'
1	School at	73350	18
2	Jo of	73650	27
3	Princess	67950	12
4	Head Girl	79500	7
5	Rivals	62200	12
6	Eustacia	74900	14
7	And Jo	54250	7
8	Camp	44650	9
9	Exploits	62500	9
10	Lintons	69650	11
11	New House	71650	17
12	Jo Returns	66400	16
13	New CS	67000	16
14	Exile	78000	15
15	Goes to it	57200	7
16	Highland Twins	81200	16
17	Lavender	77450	8
18	Gay	75800	10
19	Rescue	77350	9
19a	Mystery	23000	5
19b	Tom	48750	11
19c	Rosalie	27700	0
20	Three Go	65500	15
21	Island	71600	12
22	Peggy	75550	12

Number	Book	Word count (approx)	Mentions of 'gasp'
23	Carola	69000	14
24	Wrong	59350	8
25	Shocks	67250	9
26	CS Oberland	69550	15
27	Bride	74550	12
28	Changes	68450	15
29	Joey Oberland	61400	8
30	Barbara	71050	14
32	Does it again	68700	8
33	Kenya	68950	13
34	Mary-Lou	70750	11
35	Genius	70900	10
36	Problem	73350	14
37	New Mistress	69950	7
38	Excitements	71500	7
39	Coming of Age	70800	13
40	Richenda	69950	22
41	Trials	72500	14
42	Theodora	76900	14
43	Joey & Co	74050	13
44	Ruey	74950	9
45	Leader	61250	11
46	Wins the Trick	62700	15
47	Future	62850	10
48	Feud	59550	12
49	Triplets	62150	10
50	Reunion	59500	17
51	Jane	59800	13
52	Redheads	62050	11
53	Adrienne	59400	8
54	Summer Term	58950	16

Number	Book	Word count (approx)	Mentions of 'gasp'
55	Challenge	66350	7
56	Two Sams	60200	7
57	Althea.	50150	10
58	Prefects	50550	6

Average gasps per book: 11.6

MISS ANNERSLEY'S GASPS

Number	Book	Incident
12	Jo Returns	Margia in a sheet as Plato
13	New CS	Murdoch declines to keek at young leddies' bedrooms
25	Shocks	Commander Christy deduces that the ancient remnants are those of a bridge
27	Bride	Bride's study has been utterly wrecked
28	Changes	A sea-fog suddenly descends, cutting short the regatta
30	Barbara	Miss Annersley realises she has failed to use European time
41	Trials	Mary-Lou offers her own blood if Naomi should need a transfusion
42	Theodora	Theodora pleads to be allowed to cut all her hair off
52	Redheads	Not the gunman—Josette's engagement!

FREQUENCY OF 'THE' IN THE LAST TEN BOOKS

Number	Book	Word Count (approx)	Frequency	% to 2 dp
49	Triplets	62150	3008	4.84
50	Reunion	59500	2446	4.11
51	Jane	59800	3473	4.14
52	Redheads	62050	2914	4.70
53	Adrienne	59400	2715	4.57
54	Summer Term	58950	2885	4.90
55	Challenge	66350	3180	4.80
56	Two Sams	60200	2829	4.70
57	Althea	50150	2623	5.23
58	Prefects	50550	2731	5.41

THE TRIPLETS: RELATIVE FREQUENCY OF MENTION IN THE FINAL TEN BOOKS OF THE SERIES

Number	Book	Word Count (approx)	Len	Con	Margot
49	Triplets	62150	360	254	266
50	Reunion	59500	221	71	57
51	Jane	59800	190	36	32
52	Redheads	62050	220	25	32
53	Adrienne	59400	85	28	33
54	Summer Term	58950	138	25	32
55	Challenge	66350	118	38	127
56	Two Sams	60200	119	50	18
57	Althea	50150	220	71	46
58	Prefects	50550	207	76	76

FREQUENCY OF MENTION OF MILK, THROUGHOUT THE SERIES

Number	Book	Word count (approx)	Mentions of 'milk'
1	School at	73350	26
2	Jo of	73650	8
3	Princess	67950	7
4	Head Girl	79500	14
5	Rivals	62200	9
6	Eustacia	74900	17
7	And Jo	54250	15
8	Camp	44650	34
9	Exploits	62500	10
10	Lintons	69650	20
11	New House	71650	15
12	Jo Returns	66400	10
13	New CS	67000	21
14	Exile	78000	9
15	Goes to it	57200	8
16	Highland Twins	81200	9
17	Lavender	77450	12
18	Gay	75800	13
19	Rescue	77350	39
19a	Mystery	23000	0
19b	Tom	48750	2
19c	Rosalie	27700	9
20	Three Go	65500	10
21	Island	71600	7
22	Peggy	75550	7
23	Carola	69000	20
24	Wrong	59350	4
25	Shocks	67250	10
26	CS Oberland	69550	7

Number	Book	Word count (approx)	Mentions of 'milk'
27	Bride	74550	6
28	Changes	68450	8
29	Joey Oberland	61400	27
30	Barbara	71050	17
32	Does it again	68700	14
33	Kenya	68950	25
34	Mary-Lou	70750	16
35	Genius	70900	9
36	Problem	73350	6
37	New Mistress	69950	5
38	Excitements	71500	20
39	Coming of Age	70800	6
40	Richenda	69950	18
41	Trials	72500	10
42	Theodora	76900	8
43	Joey & Co	74050	37
44	Ruey	74950	8
45	Leader	61250	15
46	Wins the Trick	62700	7
47	Future	62850	15
48	Feud	59550	11
49	Triplets	62150	8
50	Reunion	59500	18
51	Jane	59800	6
52	Redheads	62050	11
53	Adrienne	59400	18
54	Summer Term	58950	7
55	Challenge	66350	4
56	Two Sams	60200	13
57	Althea	50150	7
58	Prefects	50550	0

Girls Gone By Publishers

Girls Gone By Publishers republish some of the most popular children's fiction from the 20th century, concentrating on those titles which are most sought after and difficult to find on the secondhand market. We aim to make them available at affordable prices, thus making ownership possible for both existing collectors and new ones so that the books continue to survive. Authors on our list include Margaret Biggs, Elinor Brent-Dyer, Dorita Fairlie Bruce, Gwendoline Courtney, Monica Edwards, Antonia Forest, Lorna Hill, Clare Mallory, Violet Needham, Elsie Jeanette Oxenham, Malcolm Saville and Geoffrey Trease. We also publish some new titles which continue the traditions of this genre.

Our series '**Fun in the Fourth—Outstanding Girls' School Stories**' has enabled us to broaden our range of authors, allowing our readers to discover a fascinating range of books long unobtainable. It features authors who only wrote one or two such books, a few of the best examples from more prolific authors (such as Dorothea Moore), and some very rare titles by authors whose other books are generally easy to find secondhand (such as Josephine Elder).

We also have a growing range of non-fiction: more general works about the genre and books on particular authors. These include *Island to Abbey* by Stella Waring and Sheila Ray (about Elsie Oxenham), *The Marlows and their Maker* by Anne Heazlewood (about Antonia Forest) and *The Monica Edwards Romney Marsh Companion* by Brian Parks. These are in a larger format than the fiction, and are lavishly illustrated in colour and black and white.

For details of availability and ordering (please do not order until titles are actually listed) go to www.ggbp.co.uk or write for a catalogue to Clarissa Cridland or Ann Mackie-Hunter, GGBP, 4 Rock Terrace, Coleford, Bath, BA3 5NF, UK.

Founded 1989

— an international fans' society founded in 1989 to foster friendship between Chalet School fans all over the world

Join Friends of the Chalet School for
Quarterly Magazines over 70 pages long
A Lending Library of all Elinor Brent-Dyer's books
Le Petit Chalet (for those aged 13 and under)
Collectors' Corner Booklets
Dustwrapper and Illustration Booklets

For more information send an A5 SAE to
Ann Mackie-Hunter or Clarissa Cridland
4 Rock Terrace, Coleford, Bath, Somerset BA3 5NF, UK
e-mail focs@rockterrace.demon.co.uk

You may also be interested in the New Chalet Club.
For further details send an SAE to
Rona Falconer, Membership Secretary,
The New Chalet Club, 18 Nuns Moor Crescent,
Newcastle upon Tyne, NE4 9BE